RELENTLESS LOVE

Hayton Monteith

A CANDLELIGHT ECSTASY ROMANCE™

Published by
Dell Publishing Co., Inc.
1 Dag Hammarskjold Plaza
New York, New York 10017

ISBN: 0-440-17188-1

Printed in the United States of America

First printing—September 1982

To Our Readers:

We have been delighted with your enthusiastic response to Candlelight Ecstasy Romances™ and we thank you for the interest you have shown in this exciting series.

In the upcoming months, we will continue to present the distinctive, sensuous love stories you have come to expect only from Ecstasy. We look forward to bringing you many more books from your favorite authors and also, the very finest work from new authors of contemporary romantic fiction.

As always, we are striving to present the unique, absorbing love stories that you enjoy most—books that are more than ordinary romance.

Your suggestions and comments are always welcome. Please write to us at the address below.

Sincerely,

The Editors
Candlelight Romances
1 Dag Hammarskjold Plaza
New York, N.Y. 10017

CHAPTER ONE

Lee Chatham replaced the phone receiver on the cradle, then put her face into her hands, her elbows resting on the desk. Alma's parting words rang in her ears like a death knell.

"You have to come out of the closet now, Rennie. You've been nominated for the Newbery Award. If you win . . ." The rest of the words faded except the first ones: "You have to come out of the closet . . ."

God, Lee thought, *if Alma only knew what she was asking of me!* She sighed and lifted her head, one hand lightly rubbing the center of her forehead. Of course, Alma was right, she thought, but not just about the book. Lee's whole life was hidden away from the public. Even Alma didn't know that Rennie Gilbert, the author of numerous children's books, was in fact Lee Chatham, the daughter of the man who had been Alma's dearest friend. No one knew what had happened to Lee Chatham. She had just disappeared, almost six years ago. Now the moment she had dreaded all that time was upon her. She had always known that something like this would happen but had closed her mind to it, willing her life and her daughter Rica's to remain constant.

Memories rushed at her, as hard as she tried to fight them, from six years ago, when she had been an untried, emotional, and naive young woman trying to cope with the loss of a beloved parent while in a foreign country.

* * *

Lee had been staying in London with her father at the home of his partner in the Chatham and Inglis publishing house, Frederick Chatham. Chad Inglis was a doting father and often took his daughter Lee Inglis with him on business trips when she was a child and after she had graduated from the small but exclusive girl's college that had also been her mother's alma mater. On one visit to the Chathams' home, Lee was laid low with a particularly nasty bout of flu. When her health began to improve, pressing business commitments called her father back to New York. It was agreed that Lee remain until she was stronger.

But the plane crashed, killing her adored father. It seemed natural for her to stay on with Frederick, turning for comfort to both him and his son, Price. Before that painful time, she hadn't had much to do with Price. He had his own flat and didn't live with his father. He was thirty-two years old to her twenty. Neither his friends nor his interests seemed to mesh with Lee's. Her reaction to his casual solicitude was an awkward shyness quite unlike the smooth, finishing school attitude she had with most people. His quizzical interest seemed piqued when, in her embarrassment at her own gaucherie, Lee began to avoid him whenever he was in Frederick's house. All at once he seemed to be around more and more. His twist of a smile was on her most of the time, his cool green eyes remote.

His father noticed Lee's agitation whenever Price was in the room and mentioned it to her. "Are you angry with Price about something, my dear?" Frederick quizzed her one day, a few months after her father's death.

"Uh . . . oh, no, Frederick. It's just that . . ." Lee gulped, her eyes filling with tears.

At once Frederick had enfolded her in his arms, his voice soothing. "It's difficult for you right now, Lee, losing your father, being in a strange country. Still, I would like you to consider Stone Manor and this flat your home for as long as you wish. I like having you here. You give this old man a great deal of comfort. As you know, Chad was my closest friend, even though he was twenty years younger than I. I'll miss him. Ah . . . but I digress." Frederick sighed. "One of the vagaries of old age, I fear. But about Price . . . dear child, you mustn't mind him. I'm sure that he must seem a hardened cynic to you. I often tell him he's too hard-bitten." He took a deep breath. "Don't be hurt by him, child!" Frederick hugged her again, then, without releasing her, he continued in a thoughtful tone. "Though I must say I have never seen him pay such singular attention to any other female . . ."

"Isn't Lee a bit young for you, Frederick?" Price's sardonic tones were amused but his eyes were cold as they raked a startled Lee from head to toe, too surprised to move from Frederick's hold at first. Neither she nor the older man had heard Price enter the room or been aware of his presence until he spoke.

"There is no need for you to be insulting, Price," Frederick began, visibly irritated by his son's remarks.

Before he could continue, Lee had fled the room, her eyes averted from Price's face.

The incident made Lee more determined to avoid Price, but her calculated efforts were met by his even more active pursuit. This was brought home to her when Price insisted on accompanying Lee and his father when they went down to Stone Manor for the week from the flat in London.

One morning as she was coming down the stairs with her swim bag, Price stopped her. "Hell . . . hello, Price. I'm just going over to Scylla's to swim." Lee hedged, feeling uncomfortable as those emerald eyes swept her from head to toe. Scylla, Price's vivacious cousin, lived a few miles away, at Bayles House. "Did you want to come with me?" She gulped.

He slowly shook his head, the hard mouth twisted in a smile. "No. I have a better idea, if it won't shock that prudish Yankee soul of yours."

Lee lifted her chin, anger at his mocking ways driving her tongue. "I'm not prudish. I'm sure I'm as game as you are."

"God, I hope not . . . but if you say so." Those arrogant black brows V-ed upward, real amusement making his eyes gleam. "Father is over at the Adams'. The house is empty. Call Scylla and tell her you can't make it. You and I will swim here. Then later we'll drive into London for dinner."

Not at any time since could Lee recall what excuse she had made to Scylla when she talked to her on the phone that morning. She could still remember with glaring clarity the feeling of the hot sun on her body when Price lowered himself next to her on the pool deck.

"Lee, baby," he crooned in her ear, amusement lacing his sardonic tones. "Lee, you're so tiny, so soft." His eyes narrowed on the quickening rise and fall of her breasts. "That blue bikini almost covers you . . . but not here . . . or here." His lips played havoc with her body, sending her first into panic, then into euphoria, then into a gentle wildness that almost matched Price's. Wrapping her arms tightly around him, she knew that she only wanted to belong to him. He pulled back first, his breathing as ragged as her own. "My little baby, not here. You really do things to me, do you know that? Come along. We'd better swim."

They had swum, and embraced and caressed each other in the water. Lee was in awe at the feelings he had so easily aroused in her. She was in wonder that the great Price Chatham seemed as interested in her as she was in him. Lee had scattered moments when she told herself she wasn't being sensible . . . then Price would take her in his arms again . . . She was lost.

That evening, she dressed in a blue cheongsam that her father had chosen for her on a trip to Taiwan. Its silkiness was like a second skin. Matching strappy sandals of pale blue and the blue beaded bag had also come from the Far

East. She had no need of a wrap in the warmth of the summer evening.

Her heels had been silenced by the plush carpet but somehow Price had sensed her entrance into the library, where he had told her he would wait for her. When he turned he was silent, but his eyes burned over her, telling her more than words could that he very much liked the way she looked.

"It's a marvelous evening," Lee offered in a breathless voice, feeling heated by his gaze. "Everyone always told me that English weather is poor, but this . . ." Lee babbled, then faltered to silence.

"You look lovely, darling. I'll be the proudest man in London tonight. Would you like a drink? No? Then I think we had better leave. It might not be a good idea to linger here," Price mocked, nibbling on her ear, laughing when she blushed.

To Lee the drive to London was heaven, the dinner was a step into paradise. She wasn't sure what it was that she ate but she was sure it was ambrosial. Champagne bubbles tickled her nose, making her giggle. When they arrived at the little club Price had talked about later in the evening, he immediately pulled her onto the dance floor. They swayed to the music as one. Lee looped both arms up to his neck, her fingers curling into his crisp black hair. Both of Price's arms were folded about her, almost lifting her from the floor. They hardly spoke but Lee could feel the pulse in his neck beating thickly against her forehead.

When they were leaving, Price's arm stayed at her waist, holding her close to him. She did not demur when he stopped at his flat and helped her from the car.

She had a hazy awareness of the ultramodern flat done in off-white and warm brown as she cupped the brandy snifter Price had placed in her hands.

"Do you like the flat, darling?" Price had whispered into her neck.

"Yes, yes. It's very . . . very sophisticated. I. . . . Don't do that Price, please," Lee begged, as she felt his lips nuzzling her ear.

"Why not, love? It feels so nice," he murmured, reaching to take the glass from her hand. "You know, you have a pretty strong head for a girl who doesn't usually drink." Price had laughed softly, setting the snifter on the coffee table; then he pressed a kiss into her palm.

"I don't like the taste of most drinks," Lee said hazily, offering no resistance as Price took her into his arms, yet feeling stiff and unsure of herself.

"Relax, love. Open your mouth, Lee. Yes, like that," Price whispered, his lips brushing back and forth across hers.

Lee felt herself drowning in sensation as his tongue touched the inside of her mouth, his fingers exploring her neck. She didn't try to stop him when she felt him loosening her dress. With a hiss of silk she was free of the gown and lifted into his arms.

She had a vague awareness that the bedroom was also in off white, then she was sinking down onto the bed, Price beside her. His probing hands set her body on fire.

"Price . . . please . . ." Lee licked dry lips, her eyelids feeling heavy.

"Shhh, love. It's our wedding night," Price had murmured, his voice thick with emotion.

"But, we're not married, Price. We mustn't . . ." Lee struggled to rally against her own mounting feeling.

"We will be, darling, soon. Lee, you have such a beautiful body," Price had growled gently, his hand stroking from thigh to breast and returning, his breathing becoming more uneven. The heat built in both of them until Lee was aware of an intolerable pressure. She sank into sensuality, the moment of pain embedded in the ecstasy.

When they were breathing normally, Lee attempted to move away from Price. A strong hand spread itself on her bare abdomen, pulling her back against Price's warm skin.

"No, Lee, don't move. We're staying the night. Tomorrow, I'll see about a special license. Hmmm, you're so soft," Price said against her cheek. He gasped when she rubbed her hand in a caressing motion down his chest and stomach. "Witch. No way are you going to sleep now."

After their lovemaking the second time, Lee sighed in contentment, curling her body into his. Sleep came almost at once. Later in the night, Price woke her, his mouth at her breast. Her body came alive at once. They turned to each other with equal hunger.

When Lee opened her eyes the next morning she could hear rain at the windows. Price was leaning over her, nuzzling her neck.

"Do you want some breakfast, sleepyhead? I've all ready been up and called Clive Ralston. In three days we'll be married at a registry office. Until then we'll stay here. Is that all right with you, Mrs. Chatham to be?" Price had teased her.

Lee nodded, after Price assured her that he would explain to Frederick.

In three days they were married, just four short months after her father's death. In easy sequence Price had taken over her life and the business from his father. They honeymooned on a yacht belonging to a friend of Price's. The Mediterranean had been perfect, their privacy total.

One evening after they returned, they joined Frederick at Stone Manor, where he was hosting a gathering of writers, editors, agents, and other publishers. Lee gave an inaudible sigh trying to keep the smile pinned to her mouth as many of the people sought her out to speak of her father. How he would have loved this, Lee thought. As senior partner in the firm, her father had been on easy terms with almost all the people present. He would have reveled in it. She took a deep breath and recalled how proud he had been of her, of her poise in dealing with his friends and business associates. She gave a rueful laugh. How different she was with Price! With him she felt ragged and in pieces, adrift yet knowing he was her anchor. She was often unable to breathe evenly in his presence. He could melt her with a look, yet make her explode in flaming temper.

"And what are you doing hiding out behind the window drapes?" Price quizzed her, his saturnine looks more defined when his eyebrows arched in amusement as she was startled from her reverie. "Not daring to dream of a secret lover, are you, child? I'll ruin him." Behind her now, he growled softly, nibbling at her ear, his arms enfolding her to him.

Irritation at his manner made her sharp with him. "Price, why must you always call me child? I'm twenty years old and your wife."

He laughed huskily, inhaling the fragrance of her hair. "Then you shouldn't be a five-foot-three-inch blonde who weighs ninety-five pounds. You shouldn't have eyes like blue quartz and thick wheat-colored hair that falls in your eyes and hangs halfway down your back."

It bothered Lee that he didn't take her question seriously, but she tried to keep her tone as light as his when she answered him. "My husband shouldn't be a tall, dark, and handsome man with lime-green eyes, then." She took a deep breath for courage, then snapped, "You look too old for me."

Lee felt him stiffen at her back, his hands tightening at her waist. His teeth nipped her neck. "The lady has claws. Do you mind the difference in our age, love?" Price's tones were flat, emotionless.

Lee had felt an instant regret for what she said. "No, no, of course not. It's just that sometimes I want to hit out at you when you laugh at me . . ."

"I don't laugh at you, my baby. If anything I'm laughing at myself . . . not you."

"What do you mean, Price? I don't understand," Lee asked him.

Price shook his head, pulling her closer. "It's not important, darling."

"See. You're doing it again, shutting me out as though I were an adolescent who wouldn't understand." Lee looked up at him, her voice urgent. "I'm a married woman, Price . . . and I'm a writer. No, don't mock me . . ."

"Love, I would never mock you . . ."

". . . because someday, I'll prove to you that I'm a writer. I'll sell more than just articles to a 'fashion rag,' as you call them. I won't need to sell to Chatham and Inglis, either. I'll make it on my own . . ." Lee paused, watching her husband's eyes lift from her and look across the room. "Price, you're not even listening to a word I say." She sighed, feeling a helpless anger at his seeming indifference to work that she not only enjoyed but also found mentally stimulating. Not for the first time she wished she could show the cool aloofness to him that he was able to show to anyone he chose. To do him justice, Lee had to admit that Price showed her flattering and constant sexual attention. He just had no regard for her as a thinking person.

Price looked back at her, his eyes heating at once. She tried to pull back and turn away but his mouth was at her temple, becoming urgent as his hands tightened under her breasts.

At once, Lee felt herself succumbing to the familiar languor. "Price, don't. Someone will see."

Price's uneven breathing steadied into the usual satiric tones, tinged with amusement. "I really don't care if they do."

"No." Lee twisted free, anger touching her when she couldn't control her own breathing. She had the feeling he was teasing her again. How she hated being so vulnerable to his every mood. Her love for him had made her raw, open to hurt. She took a deep gulp of air to steady herself. "Frederick will want us to entertain his guests. They are your guests as well, Price."

Price smiled, flicking her cheek with one strong finger. "All right, child, don't look so prim." A thoughtful look came over his face. "By the way, angel, I'll be going back to London tonight. I'll drive in with Felice and Aslind Harvey. I'll be back on Wednesday."

"But, Price," she wailed, not wanting him to leave her, "I was going to drive up to London with Scylla tomorrow and do some shopping. Couldn't you drive in with us?"

Price kissed her nose, shaking his head. "I have to be in the office early, so I'll stay at the flat tonight. Don't fret, my baby. Drive in on Wednesday and I'll come back with you. If you need money for shopping, there's plenty in the safe."

Frustrated, Lee caught at the hands enclosing her face. "I don't need money, Price. You always give me too much."

"I could never give you too much of anything," Price growled softly. "Don't you know that by now, angel?" He laughed, kissed her once, hard, and walked away to join a group of men who were beckoning to him.

The next day, Scylla was insistent that they not change their shopping-trip plans. "Darling Lee, you give in too much to Price, far too much. That sexy cousin of mine is far too bossy. I insist you come with me. I must pick up those shoes at Lucio's for the dinner party on Wednesday."

Lee succumbed to Scylla's urging, exhilarated at the prospect of a day's shopping . . . and maybe seeing Price.

The all-day trudging through the stores with the irrepressible Scylla had been fruitful and tiring. Lee never had a chance to call Price and tell him she was in London.

Scylla exhaled an exhausted breath. "Lee, I don't know about you but I can't face that drive back to Bayles House tonight. How about staying with me at father's flat? We'll drive back in the morning."

Lee shook her head, a smile of anticipation on her face. "Thanks, but I think that I'll stay at our flat as long as Price is here in town. I'll pick you up at seven sharp in the morning. That should get you back in plenty of time for your nine o'clock tennis lesson. You and the handsome Jocko make quite a team." Lee laughed.

"Don't we, though?" Scylla said saucily before laughing with Lee. Both girls were twenty and life was sweet.

They dined at a Chinese restaurant noted for its food. Lee had remembered that Price would probably have a dinner engagement with a colleague or two the first evening back in town. She decided not to call at all. She would surprise him later in the evening.

Lee had been whistling soundlessly as she let herself into the flat, a little after ten that evening. She had a vague notion that the low feminine laughter she heard must be coming from the television. She knew that the male voice she heard was Price's. She ambled along the thick pile-carpeted hallway to their bedroom. Figuring that she had enough light from the lamp in the lounge, she didn't bother to switch on the hall light. Lee was in comparative darkness to the muted light from the bedroom. The two figures clasped together didn't notice her. The roaring in Lee's ears prevented her from hearing any of the words the other two might have spoken. Felice Harvey was wrapped in a towel. Price was dressed, but his shirt was unbuttoned to his belt. He was looking down at Felice, his hands on her shoulders.

Lee turned without a sound and left the apartment. She drove around London, not noticing where she was going. Fatigue made her find a hotel, but still she couldn't sleep. She paced the boxlike room until morning. At six in the morning, a cold, withdrawn Lee showered, not caring that she had neither toothbrush nor change of clothes.

Picking up Scylla a little after seven, she drove back to Bayles House through a gray morning mist, trying to make the appropriate responses to the other girl's chatter.

"Didn't you sleep well, Lee?" Scylla interrupted her own seething dissertation on cleaning women to be found in London to quiz Lee. "That beast Price—did he keep you up all night? You do look a little pale, love."

Lee knew her laugh sounded harsh but she ignored the sharp-eyed look Scylla gave her.

When they curved up the half-moon drive and stopped at the front door of Bayles House, Lee turned to Scylla, a catch in her throat. "Take care, won't you, Scylla. Don't call me before Thursday, please."

"Why? What's wrong?" Scylla asked, a frown on her face.

"Nothing. I might be going back to London. I'll call you when I return," Lee stated flatly. She waved and drove away, not looking back.

Once at Stone Manor, Lee went first to the wall safe in the library, after being informed by Mrs. Wigg, the housekeeper, that her father-in-law had decided to spend a couple of days with his friends the Adamses. As usual, there was a great deal of cash in the safe, both American dollars and British pound notes. Price hated the bother of trying to change money at the last minute, and since he spent a great deal of time in America it suited him to keep large amounts of cash on hand. Lee stuffed her purse with both dollars and pound notes, reaching at the same time for her passport.

She left Price a note, which she placed in the safe, explaining that she was leaving him, that he could deduct the money she was taking from her shares of stock in Chatham and Inglis. She also asked him not to try to find her, that she needed time alone to get her life in order. She left another note for her father-in-law telling him how much she loved him but that she found it impossible to stay with Price.

Lee was sure that she would have the opportunity to disappear, because Price wouldn't check the safe right away. Just to cover her tracks even more, she left another note for Price in their bedroom telling him she was staying with Scylla and that she would return on Friday.

When she had landed in New York, her first thought had been to contact her father's dear friend, Alma McInerny, who was the head of Travers Literary Agents, Inc. Lee could still remember the panic that had changed her mind. The need to hide was greater than the need to unburden to a friend.

Almost by instinct she used her mother's maiden name of Gilbert when she bought a plane ticket to Rochester, New York. Once there she hired a car to drive the thirty-five or forty miles to her mother's childhood home in the Bristol Hills.

While her mother was still living the original homestead had burned down. A rambling one-story frame house in the shape of the letter H, lying lengthwise, had been erected. Though her father had never wanted to live there after her mother had died, the quite modern house was kept in excellent repair. A close childhood friend of her mother's by the name of Gladys Ogilvie, widowed with no children of her own, lived there and acted as housekeeper. Tom Wiggins, another local, had been a friend of her mother's family's for years and now acted as caretaker for the small vineyard on the grounds that sold grapes to the nearby wineries. The house sat atop a high knoll with a winding road that led to the small crystal-clear lake below. The holding included a long stretch of shale beach on which was built a dock and cabana for changing.

Lee smiled to herself as she recalled the warm welcome Gladdy had given her, the unquestioning affection that kept her talking about Lee's mother, not the shadows in Lee's eyes. "Of course, you don't remember this but I can still hear your mother saying if you were a boy you would be called Leroy after your grandfather Gilbert. When you turned out to be a girl, she decided to call you the feminine of Leroy, which was La Reine, meaning the queen. It just seemed to shorten itself to Lee."

Lee swallowed some of the juice that had gone tepid in the glass and thought how she had pondered on the last part of her first name when she began writing children's fiction in earnest. She had decided to use the pen name of Rennie Gilbert. She sighed, remembering more.

After she had been at Highland Farms for a few weeks she was able to tell Gladdy some of the reasons she had left Price. She realized now that the pain she felt when she mentioned Felice Harvey's name must have shown on her face and told Gladdy far more than words.

Writing became Lee's solace. Words had flowed from her, easing her pain. Days turned into weeks, weeks into months. Her fears about her thickening waist, dizzy spells, and morning nausea crystallized. She could still recall how she had reached out to Gladdy, afraid.

"Oh, Gladdy, what should I do?" Lee's fearful question was answered with country logic and sense.

"First, we'll see Doctor Spellman at the medical center. He's my family doctor. He'll know a good obstetrician," Gladdy had soothed.

Dr. Webber had been a good obstetrician. "Well, Mrs. Chatham, you're in fine shape," he had opined. "Though in my opinion you're a a little narrow through the hips to be a first class breeder, to put it in horse country vernacular." He twinkled at her over his half-glasses. "Don't like horses, myself. I fall off." When Lee laughed he patted her hand. "Good. I like my mothers to be happy . . . not have shadows in their eyes. Now, I don't mind the slimness too much but I do insist that you take your vitamins and exercise judiciously. Don't take on weightlifting but keep up the swimming and running. I'll see you in a month."

The forty-five-minute return ride to the knolltop home was nearly completed before Gladdy spoke. "Lee, honey, shouldn't you get in touch with your husband . . . ?"

"No. No, I can't do that. I won't do it, ever." Lee could feel hysteria rising like bile in her throat and bit down on her lip. "He doesn't care for me. He thinks I'm a pesty child. I should think having two children would be too much for him. Why would he want my baby and me?" Lee asked, her voice wobbling. "I'll have my baby, take care of it myself. I'm writing more now. We'll get along just fine. Please, Gladdy, try to understand. I just can't get in touch with Price."

"All right. All right." Gladdy lifted one hand from the wheel and patted Lee's knee, trying to placate her. "The three of us will manage very well."

In a few short months the children's book she had been writing was finished. Crossing her fingers, she sent it to Alma McInerny, using her pen name of Rennie Gilbert. She couldn't bring herself to reveal her true identity to Alma, though she felt guilty fooling a woman who had shown her only kindness and affection in the past. Lee still had the strong urge to remain hidden, but besides that she had a strong wish to try her work out on the marketplace without the cachet that her father's name would give her. She also knew that Alma would have bent over backward for her if she had an inkling as to who she was.

Six weeks later, Alma sent a terse note, saying she would take on Rennie Gilbert's first work, *Walk on the Bright Side.* She gave no guarantees but she had a feeling it might go. *Walk* sold to the fifth publishing house to which Alma had sent it. The eleven-year-old heroine, a carbon copy of Lee at the same age, became a well-known personage. The book sold well to libraries, and Lee was buoyed by her success. When Alma informed her that she had been approached about making the book into a movie, Lee was overwhelmed.

"Now, you should come to New York, Rennie," Alma urged. "There are any number of publicity angles we could cover. Say you'll come."

"No, Alma, I'm not coming. I value my privacy and don't want to be in the limelight. Let my books speak for me. You handle the business end for me. Besides I have another . . . uh . . . commitment coming up."

Lee's baby, Frederica Price Chatham, was born in early spring, before the movie was made. Her publisher never knew that Lee's book was not the most important thing in her life.

Royalties began filling the coffers of Highland Farms, Inc., which consisted of Lee, Gladdy, and Rica.

Lee's second book was equally well received. The small family was making it. The baby, Rica, brought much needed joy and laughter into the household.

"Lee, you're very good with Rica," Gladdy said, smiling at the gurgling baby one crisp spring day. "I think some folks around here would be surprised to see the aloof Mrs. Chatham rolling on the floor with her baby girl."

Lee's face was still, her eyes searching Gladdy's face. "Am I aloof, Gladdy? I don't mean to be. It's just that . . ." Lee shrugged, looking at the other woman with a helpless look on her face.

"I know, I know. It's difficult for you . . . but your reserved ways are alien to the people around here . . ." Gladdy stopped, her eyes widening on Rica. "Oh, look at that, she has a tooth," Gladdy crowed.

Lee clasped her daughter to her, cooing over the new tooth. "Isn't she gorgeous, Gladdy? All those dark curly wisps all over her head and those big green eyes. She's so like Pr . . . the Chathams." Lee gulped, blinking fast. Lee was careful not to mention Price too often. It hurt too much . . . but every time she looked at the baby, she could see him. To Lee, Rica was the image of her father.

She was grateful that Gladdy had never mentioned contacting Price after that first time. The thought of seeing him almost made Lee physically ill. No, she had promised herself, she would keep the peace of mind that she had found at Highland Farms. Rica was all the excitement and happiness she would ever need.

A painful stab of guilt interrupted Lee's reverie as she thought of Frederick and how she was denying him his right to see his granddaughter. How Rica would love that gentle man.

When she rose to leave her study and inform Gladdy of her decision, she took a deep breath and stiffened her shoulders, an unconscious habit that had become part of her personality in the last six years. She would accept Alma's offer. She would come out of the closet. But people would find they were no longer dealing with a tremulous twenty-year-old who was unwilling to deal with her own destiny.

Lee's chin came up as she thought of Price. He would see just how tough she could be. For a second she quailed as she thought of her husband's almost ruthless single-mindedness, which Frederick had so often shaken his head over. He assured Lee that it must have come from his Greek mother, since her brothers were in shipping and handled all their opposition with lethal dispatch. At the time Lee had laughed with him. Now she shuddered as she thought of the consequences of her decision. Price would want her back. Certainly he would want his daughter. A man like him would not have taken her desertion lightly. God only knew what he would do. But Lee would face him down, whatever the cost. She had to—for her sake and for Rica's.

Sighing, she went down the hall to the kitchen, pausing at a window to watch Rica and her friend Johnny Greenway wrestle with Duke, the huge coal-black Newfoundland whose coat echoed Rica's shiny ebony curls. The child and dog were constant companions. Lee smiled as she watched them. This was enough of life for her and she would fight for it. Let Price keep his women.

My books are selling well, Lee thought, itemizing her blessings in her mind. *Walk on the Bright Side* was being made into a mini-series on TV and now there was the Newbery Award nomination. Lee's smile widened as she thought of Alma McInerny's frustrated urgings for her to come to New York. Lee had never revealed herself to her agent. They talked on the phone, with Lee doing the calling. All Alma's correspondence was addressed to a post office box in Honeoye Falls, New York.

Even my social life isn't that bad, Lee mused as she retrieved some of Rica's crayons from the hall floor. She thought of Grant Lieber with a sigh. He was an acquaintance dating back to her childhood summers on the lake. He began to call Lee when he saw her in town one day when she was at the post office. She had dated Grant when she was a teen-ager, even though he was five years older than she. She remembered how flattered she had been by his attention.

"Lee, you've become a very sophisticated woman. I like that," he had told her one night when they were returning from a band concert at the local high school. Grant's niece played clarinet in the orchestra.

"Thank you, Grant." Lee's smile was rueful as she recalled the way Price had always called her "child." It still rankled her. "But I'm sure you would never think me sophisticated if you saw me in the company of some of the career women that I knew in New York and London."

"Well, they wouldn't interest me," Grant stated firmly. "You're just right for me and the kind of life I want. I'm sure you understand me, Lee?"

When Grant had kissed her, Lee had pressed herself against him, feeling a mild stirring in her from the pressure of his kiss. She was satisfied.

Taking a deep breath, she shook herself from her reverie and walked into the kitchen, sitting her self on a high stool and beginning to arrange crisp spinach leaves in a wooden salad bowl.

Gladdy lifted one eyebrow but said nothing.

"Gladdy," Lee said, munching on a small piece of lettuce. "That was Alma on the phone. I've been nominated for the Newbery Award." Lee held up her hand, forestalling Gladdy's comment. "It's good in one way . . . but . . . Alma wants me in New York."

"You're going," Gladdy stated laconically.

"Yes. I'm coming out of my corner . . . and I'm coming out swinging, Gladdy. I have no illusions. I know that Price will know almost at once when I show myself—the publishing world is a tight-knit circle—but . . . it's time." Lee coughed at the sudden dryness in her throat. "Rica is almost five. She's growing up. She should know her father and her grandfather. . . ."

"It's time, all right. She's beginning to look on Grant Lieber as a father figure," Gladdy said, wiping damp hands on a towel. "It seems to me that if you're marrying Grant, it's all right for Rica to feel that way . . . but you're still married to Price Chatham. Now, don't get that stiff-chin, stiff-shoulder look. I'm on your side, remember?"

Lee nodded, shrugging. "He wants to marry me, Gladdy."

"If you care for him, do it, Lee. You deserve some happiness." Gladdy pursed her lips in a mannerism that was familiar to Lee. "The Liebers are a prominent family in these parts. Grant's aunt Lilly was at school with your mother and me. They make all the right moves. You know what I mean . . . yacht club, country club, active in community affairs . . ." Gladdy ticked off the items on her fingers as though she were reenforcing her words. "Grant is a successful lawyer. He dotes on Rica—in fact, sometimes I think he's almost too . . . oh, well, it's not important. He would certainly stand between you and Price Chatham. He would gladly handle your divorce and follow it through to the end . . ." Gladdy's voice dwindled a little in strength as she noticed Lee stiffening. Then she swallowed and gave her head a determined shake. She plowed forward, her voice sounding harsh. "Lee, Price Chatham isn't part of your life now. At least, that's the way you seem to want it . . ."

"I do." Lee spoke curtly, her hands clenched at her sides.

"Then . . . it's time you did something constructive about making the break final. He lives in England, doesn't he?" Gladdy pressed onward as Lee nodded a yes. "Well, for all you know . . . I mean, maybe he has divorced you and remarried. That's a possibility."

Lee gulped, her head giving an unconscious shake. "No. I don't think so. The divorce laws are still pretty tight over there, Gladdy, and I think even with the Enoch Arden law in force, I wouldn't think he had gotten one. You need seven years for that." Lee gripped her hands together in painful intensity. "I don't know. What can I say about what Price has done these past years? I know nothing. Oh, Gladdy, I'm almost afraid to start anything. I can't lose Rica."

The older woman moved forward, her one hand clasping Lee's shoulder. "You won't lose her, Lee. Grant will see to that. Even stuffed-shirt lawyers have their uses," she pointed out wryly.

Lee gave a reluctant laugh. "Gladdy, Grant isn't a stuffed shirt. Perhaps he's a little on the conservative side . . . but . . ." Lee shrugged.

"Balderdash, as my grandpa used to say . . . but the important thing is that you like him. I won't say any more against him." She made a moue at Lee's skeptical glance. "There is one other thing, while we're on the subject. Do you remember mentioning that Alma McInerny was having another one of those cocktail parties that she's always having?" At Lee's quizzical nod, Gladdy hitched her apron higher on her hips. "Well, I was thinking, it might not be a bad idea to attend this one. She's always wanting you to come. Maybe now's the time. Make yourself known to her, Lee. She was so very fond of your father. She'll help you, I feel it. I can't see her being afraid of Chatham . . ."

"She's not afraid of anyone." Lee laughed.

"Well, there you are. Do it, Lee. Go to New York. You have to come out in the open, Lee," Gladdy urged.

"Why do I have the feeling I'm being steam-rollered?" Lee sighed. "I suppose you're right." She put her arms around the other woman, hugging her. Then she stepped back, looking at her. Not for the first time, Lee thought what an attractive woman she must have been in her early years, her figure still neat and trim, her tall angular looks crowned by a thick white swirl of short hair. "You're right," Lee repeated. "Nothing can be done until I begin divorce proceedings. Maybe going to see Alma will kill two birds with one stone. I can sign the contract for *Penguin Stories.*" Lee's smile wobbled as a sudden picture of Price intruded itself into her thoughts. What would it be like to see him again? She couldn't rid herself of the vague, nagging fear. Price was a man who took what he wanted. Would she have the strength to stand up to him finally? As a woman? As an equal? She remembered how he had treated her like little more than a precious pet and shivered. She was a different woman now. She had proven her independence and her strength. The frightened young girl who needed the comfort and protection of his arms no longer existed. She had died when Lee saw how free those arms could be. The protection died, the comfort died, the love died.

She brought her thoughts back to the woman in front of her. "I think I'll go for a swim before Rica wakens. Grant is coming to dinner. I'll talk to him then about a divorce."

"You can't go swimming yet. It's only May. You'll freeze," Gladdy yelped.

Lee took a deep breath and turned away. She had to be alone for a while to think things through. She would be divorced . . . free of Price. That's what she wanted, wasn't it? She'd waited long enough. Divorce was the only answer. It took mere minutes to change into a one-piece suit and grab a toweling jacket and towel.

She kicked at the stones that lined the curving drive leading from the house in a downward sweep from the bluff to the beach. The sun was hot. Lee's eyes were not soothed as they usually were by the rows of grapevines that stretched up the hill to the crest in undulating rows for almost two miles. Highland Farms, though not a large holding, was a paying operation. Lee was proud of their grapes and of the contract they had with The Silver Lining Wine Company. Next year they would be putting more land to vines. Lee was sure the profits would grow, however slowly. She would insure both Rica's and her own future. They would be independent.

The beach didn't have its usual balming effect, either. Lee felt restless, uncertain. She let her eyes rove across the lake to the other side, noting idly the farm tractor working the hill on the other side, looking more like a toy at such a distance. She looked down the almost quarter mile of beach front that belonged to Highland Farms and blessed the foresight of her father, who had insisted on purchasing it when he had rebuilt the house.

The water was breath-catching cold. Lee wondered if she would be able to dip her body as she longed to do. Glancing down the front of her sky-blue Lycra suit, she could see the goose bumps on her thighs. Taking a deep breath she immersed herself, coming up gasping but unwilling to come out until she had tried to swim a few strokes. Gritting her teeth, she swam up and down a few times, coming out of the water a few moments later with almost no feeling whatever in her legs. She felt cleansed and refreshed . . . less anxious. Vigorous toweling dried and calmed her even more.

It was very possible that Price would be at Alma's party; after all, Price and Alma knew each other. Her moment of truth could come that soon. But she'd be able to handle it, she adjured herself, folding her towel. No matter what occurred she would deal with it. No doubt she should marry Grant. Rica needed a father, and it was obvious that Rica liked Grant.

Shaking back her still-wet hair, Lee forced herself to run up the hilly drive so that she would be out of breath.

She often used strenuous exercise to blot out memories that she couldn't suppress.

Would her lovemaking with Grant be like it had been with Price? The thought sprang, unbidden, to her mind. "Oh, God," she gasped out loud, her heartbeats sounding loud in her ears as she forced herself to greater speed, *why must I think of that now? I'm not going to think of stupid things like that,* she moaned to herself. She gave her head a vigorous shake, trying to blot such thoughts from her memory. Her body felt suddenly hot. No, no, no, she wouldn't think of them together. She flogged herself with mental pictures of Price and Felice as she had seen them in the apartment.

As soon as she reached the house she headed for the shower, standing under it long minutes to let the needles of spray work their tranquilizing effects. She shampooed her head with ruthless massaging fingers.

After dinner that evening, she watched Grant push Rica on the big wooden swing that Tom Wiggins had suspended from the giant oak in the yard. *What would it have been like if it were Price here now, instead of Grant, pushing their child high into the air?* The thought startled Lee, making her feel unsettled. She pushed herself out of the wicker chair so quickly that the chair wobbled precariously before righting itself. "Please, Grant, don't push her quite so high. It could be dangerous." Lee's voice was unsteady.

"Don't fuss, dear," Grant stated, not looking back at Lee. "You like being pushed high, don't you, Rica? Ah, I knew you did. That's my girl."

Rica tilted her head back, laughing. Her hand slipped on the thick braided rope. Lee jumped forward, catching the child as she started to fall. The seat of the swing caught Lee on the hip, striking her hard.

Rica began to cry in reaction to the sudden commotion. Lee held her, gritting her teeth at the sharp pain in her hip.

While she was still crooning comfortingly to the little girl, Grant swept her from Lee's arms, then lifted her high in the air, stopping her tears.

"Big girls don't cry, Rica." Grant laughed at her. When Lee went to reach for Rica, he lifted the child away. "No, no, Lee, let me handle this," he insisted. "You would only get her crying again by giving her too much sympathy. That's my big girl." He turned to look at Rica. Soon the child was laughing again.

Later in the evening, after Rica was tucked in for the night and Gladdy had retired to her own apartment over the garage, Lee discussed her tentative plans with Grant. "Of course, I don't know for sure if he will be at Alma's but she will know how to contact him." Lee twisted her hands together. "And I'm sure once he knows where I am he'll contact me." Contact isn't the right word, Lee thought to herself wryly. He'll probably roar like a lion and knock down a few buildings.

"Lee? Lee, what are you thinking that's put such a fierce look on your face?" Grant quizzed her, his face creased in a frown.

"What? Oh, pardon me, Grant. It was nothing. So, you really think it would be a good idea for me to go to New York?"

"Of course I do. The sooner we get the ball rolling the sooner you'll be free. Then we'll be able to make plans for our own life." Grant smiled, leaning toward her and enfolding her in his arms.

Lee closed her eyes, enjoying the warm feeling Grant gave her. No more would she seek the kind of thrilling excitement she'd felt with Price. It would be the safe road all the way for her and for Rica.

"Lee, what do you say to planning our wedding for a year from now? I'm sure you'll be free at that time. It will be the biggest event in the Bristols next year . . ." Grant gloated, not even noticing when Lee edged away from his embrace.

"Grant, I don't want a big wedding. I don't think I'd feel right about that. After all, I have been married before . . . and . . . well, I would feel uncomfortable planning . . ."

"Don't worry about the planning, Lee. My sister Tansy will plan everything. She knows just how these things should be done." Grant rolled on, seemingly buoyed by the very idea. "We'll have Rica for flower girl . . ."

"No. No, I will not allow it, Grant. Rica will not be in the wedding," Lee stated firmly, her hand shaking a little as she put it to her head.

"Really, dear, you're being foolish. You're worrying about something that doesn't matter at all, your first marriage. Just discount it as a bad experience, Lee. You weren't married long enough for it to matter to you. So forget it," Grant said, sounding slightly affronted by her adamant stand on Rica.

Lee didn't care. She wasn't going to budge on that point. "Grant, it may seem like nothing to you . . . but that nothing produced Rica and so it does mean something to me. I will take no chance on subjecting Rica to gossip. I mean that."

"All right, Lee," Grant sighed. "Well, I think you should make plans to get to New York right away," Grant said loftily. "In the meantime I will be setting the wheels in motion for the divorce. I don't think any judge will find for Chatham. The man's a lecher," Grant said with courtroom finality.

Lee almost smiled at the archaic term, lecher. "He isn't really like that, Grant. Women chased him, yes, but . . ."

"And I'm sure he didn't try to escape. Don't defend him, Lee. Look how unhappy he made you. That kind of man would always make a woman unhappy," he said, his tones unequivocal.

He didn't make them unhappy all the time, Lee thought, feeling herself redden with embarrassment at the thought.

She lifted her chin, feeling awkward. "I'm not defending him. It's just that . . . oh, never mind. The only important thing is that I keep Rica. She's my life."

"*We'll* keep her, dear," Grant remarked sententiously.

Lee walked him to the door to say good night. She barely took notice of his kiss. The one thought in her mind was that she would keep Rica safe no matter what the cost.

CHAPTER TWO

At the Hyatt Hotel in New York City, Lee signed the register Rennie Gilbert. She called Alma as soon as she had unpacked. "Alma? Yes, I mean it. No, I won't change my mind. Alma, I'd like to come a little early, if I may. I want to talk to you."

That night she took special pains with her toilet, brushing blue eye shadow across her lids, touching her lips with the same pale coral that colored her nails. Her dress was a black silk that clung to her petite figure like another skin . . . until she moved. Then the inverted pleats flared, emphasizing her slim legs. Spaghetti straps held the tight bodice. Her four-inch peau de soie strap sandals were black as well, the extra height giving her an added confidence. Her blond hair was carefully coiled in a style that defined the delicacy of her high cheekbones and enhanced the translucent quality of her skin. She wore small drop diamond earrings that had belonged to her mother and a matching diamond pinkie ring. She wore no other jewelry. When she had finished dressing she studied her image in the mirror, turning this way and that to assure herself that the tiny catch in her extremely sheer nylons did not show. Then, throwing a hand-crocheted lace stole over her shoulders, she took a deep breath and left the room.

At 6:55, her hand shaking, Lee rang the bell at Alma's apartment. The door was opened by Alma herself.

"So . . . you're Rennie Gilbert. I expected you to be older. Come in, come in." Alma smiled and stepped back.

Lee saw the other woman's eyes widen as she stepped into the foyer. "Do I know you? I do, don't I? Have we met at a literary function? Mystery Writers, maybe? I get the feeling I knew you not as a children's author," Alma mused, leading her through the lounge area and down a short hall. "Ah, here we are. This is my study. We've only half an hour, I'm sorry to say. Sit down, sit down. Right there is fine. Now tell me where we've met."

Lee settled herself into the leather chair near the desk and gave a small smile. "We met at the Southampton Sail Club when I was fourteen. We met many times after that, sometimes at those literary functions you mentioned."

In the act of lowering her medium height, sausage frame into the chair behind the desk, Alma paused and stared. Her cigarette in the carved ivory holder fell onto the desk. She picked it up at once, not taking her eyes from Lee. "No . . . you can't be. Lee Inglis? I mean, Lee Chatham? You've been missing for . . . what is it now? Five years? No, it's more than that. You disappeared. Now you appear as Rennie Gilbert? What is going on? My God, I can't believe this."

"I had to be by myself." Lee smiled weakly at Alma's stunned look.

"I don't understand any of this," Alma whispered, fumbling with her lighter that wouldn't ignite. "Where have you been, Lee? No, that's stupid. You've been in Honeoye Falls, New York, wherever the hell that is. That's where your post office box is, anyway," Alma muttered almost to herself. Then her head lifted. She stared at Lee fixedly. "Lord, girl, Price may be here tonight. He often comes here when he's in New York . . . and he has been in New York a great deal since your disappearance. He's never spoken of you to me but I've had the feeling he has never stopped looking for you. I don't know his feelings about you either . . . but I can tell you that he's a dangerous adversary. I wouldn't like to cross him."

"I know," Lee said grimly.

"Ah . . . all right. Did you know that Frederick has been ill? He's better now. He was in the Bahamas for a while, recovering . . ." Alma sank back in her swivel chair, answering Lee's searching questions about Frederick. All at once the two women were silent, both visibly shaken by their meeting. Alma rubbed her right forefinger across her upper lip, her mouth not quite steady.

Lee cleared her throat but there was still a slight quaver in her voice when she resumed speaking. "I'm sorry to have shocked you like this, Alma, but, as you said to me on the phone, it was time to come out of the closet . . ." Lee sketched very thinly the past six years, making it clear to Alma that she intended to start divorce proceedings if Price had not all ready done so.

Alma shook her head at that, saying that Price had not divorced her, as far as she knew. She put another cigarette into the ivory holder. "I'm going to smoke another one of these awful things. I need it." She shrugged at Lee. "Hardly ever smoke at my parties anymore. Too damned many environmentalists . . . nag me to death." She tried to smile at Lee but her lips trembled. She looked down at her cigarette. "You're like him, Lee, do you know that? Very, very like him. God, but I still miss him. Your father was the world to me." She inhaled deeply and shot a sharp-eyed look at Lee. "Be careful, Lee. Price could get very . . . rough. I'm not so ignorant that I don't know you've changed from the girl I knew . . . but don't be foolish enough to think you can handle Price. He can be pretty scary." She gave a rueful grin. "But whatever you do decide to do, I'll help you. You're all of Chad I have left." Alma lifted her head, looking toward the door, listening. "That sounds like the first guests arriving. Stay here for a moment, if you like. Come out when you choose. There's brandy on that sideboard, if you need it."

Lee didn't take any brandy. She just leaned back in her chair after Alma departed and closed her eyes. She felt drained.

She must have dozed, for something startled her awake. The party was in full swing. Lee studied her image in the small mirror over the sideboard, smoothing back a strand of blond hair that had loosened while she slept. She was too pale, she had to admit, shading a touch of blusher onto her cheeks. With a too-tight grip on her clutch purse, she stepped into the hall and followed it to the door of the lounge. She was assailed by the too-loud laughter and the clink of glasses. Her first nervous scan of the room told her Price wasn't there. Her upper lip was beaded with nervous moisture. She chided herself for being a fool and thought of Rica and the good life they had. It made her stiffen her spine and thrust back her shoulders. She took a deep breath and searched the room again, knowing Price wasn't there. She could picture his tall, broad-shouldered body, the cold yet intense green eyes, the saturnine smile that creased the craggy face into surprising dimples, which gave his face an almost frightening sensuality. She inhaled sharply when she noticed a man with similar black hair, the tight curls cut medium short. She jumped when a voice spoke close to her ear.

"Hello. I haven't seen you here before, have I? I'm Steve Blaylock of Hardesty and Curran."

Lee smiled at the open-faced man standing in front of her. She was intrigued. Hardesty and Curran owned Apple House, the publishing house that handled her books. She put out her hand. "I'm Rennie Gilbert. How do you do."

Steve Blaylock's hand hesitated just a moment, his eyes narrowing. "*The* Rennie Gilbert? Newbery nominee Gilbert? Author of *Walk on the Bright Side* and *Lace Curtain Summer?*"

"Yes to all three questions." Lee smiled.

His eyes touched her from head to foot. "Wow, nice combination. Talent and looks." His leer was friendly. "Somehow I always pictured you as being older. By the way, I think Cynthia Wellman is coming tonight. Are you here to see her? She'll be jubilant." Steve got Lee a highball and returned to answer all her questions about her editor at Apple House in a relaxed way. "By the way, did you know that H and C is merging with Chatham and Inglis?"

Lee could feel her nails digging into her palms. "No. No, I didn't know that, Mr. Blaylock." She turned away, not wanting him to see the shock she knew must be showing on her face. The movement made her dress billow out around her, revealing her legs, and a strange sound escaped from Blaylock's throat. When she looked back at him, there was an appreciative glint in his eye and his sandy-colored good looks had taken on a rakish air.

Lee relaxed, letting herself enjoy the mildly flirtatious vibrations between them, when a deep laugh and a light bustle at the door made her stiffen. All at once breathing was difficult. She looked over Steve's shoulder to the mirror above the mantel.

It surprised Lee that Price was still larger than life, that the legacy of his Greek mother could be even more pronounced. The gleaming emerald eyes were more jewellike, harder. The hair curled in a deep anthracite black, emphasized by the silver touches that Lee didn't remember. An unruly curl still fell onto his forehead, an incredibly boyish manifestation on that ruggedly handsome face. It irked Lee that he should still be the most blatantly masculine man she had ever known. With restless eyes that seemed glued to the mirror she watched other women respond to his presence. At once bored expressions were replaced by an avid glitter that made Lee clench her hands. Lazy stances were corrected into breast-high, stomach-in postures. To Price's credit, Lee admitted begrudgingly, he seemed unaware that he was the center of feminine attention. She swallowed in a suddenly dry throat as she realized that she was in the same room with her husband whom she had not seen nor spoken to in six years.

A tinkling laugh pulled Lee's eyes from Price to his

companion. Her first thought was that the laugh didn't fit the Juno-esque redhead who clung to her husband's arm, her voluptuous charms enhanced by a low-cut turquoise satin dress that left little to the imagination. Lee swallowed in irritation, angry with herself for being so stupid. He probably had several more stunning women in the wings waiting for the crook of his finger. Women had always chased him.

"Ah, I see what has taken your attention," Steve Blaylock whispered, turning to catch the images in the mirror, then looking back to the door, a knowing smile on his face. "The lovely Darvi Lindquist in all her . . . ah . . . splendor. Much like the prow of a ship is our Darvi. Comes on a little strong . . . but very sexy. I see she has her usual squire of late, our dynamic boss to be. I wonder how long Darvi will last. Price Chatham isn't known for being the most faithful of men . . . Hey, Rennie, are you all right? You look pale . . ."

Lee looked for a minute at Steve, trying to smile, trying not to let him see how much his remark had torn at her. Then she looked back at the mirror, as though her eyes had a will of their own.

In an old familiar gesture, Price tugged at his shirt cuff. Of course, the crease in his black-green silk suit was knife sharp. *Impeccably dressed as ever,* Lee thought on a quivering breath.

Price released Alma from the hug he had given her, laughing at something she said. He let his eyes sweep the room, almost at once catching Lee's in the mirror. His casual smile froze on lips suddenly drawn thin and cruel. Icy green eyes fixed upon her, and Lee felt the room recede. She and Price were alone.

"Rennie, Rennie, what is it? You're white again. Are you ill . . . in pain?" Steve quizzed her, concerned, one hand cupping her elbow, turning her to face him.

Yes, I'm ill and I'm in pain, Lee felt like shouting. It was as though she had just emerged from a frigid lake

. . . tingling but numb. "No, I'm not ill. Thank you, Steve. I'm fine. Perhaps . . ."

Before she could finish, Steve's puzzled gaze lifted from her face to stare over her head, his face relaxing in a smile. Lee clutched her glass with both hands to still their trembling.

"Price, Price Chatham, how are you?" Steve took an outstretched hand that was close to Lee's arm. "Have you met Rennie Gilbert? No? Price, this is Rennie. Rennie, this is Price Chatham."

Lee turned, her skirt swishing in a soft arc around her legs, her right hand outstretched. Price's hand was as large and warm—as she remembered it. She kept her eyes level with his tie clip. "How do you do."

"Rennie Gilbert," Price rasped, his voice harsher than she remembered. "So you're she." Price paused, lifting his head, an irritated look on his face. "What? Oh, pardon me, Steve. Yes, I'll have a whiskey and soda, Irish if they have it, no ice. Miss Gilbert?"

"Ah . . . I think I'll go with Steve. I'd prefer something other than another highball," Lee stated, wanting to escape the consequences of her husband's icy rage, at least for the moment.

The hand on her arm, stilling her, was like steel, the voice raw silk. "Don't go . . . Miss Gilbert." The green ice floe eyes cut into her, almost making her shudder. "Of course you don't want whiskey."

Lee gritted her teeth, raising her chin a little, knowing she would have a bruise on her arm in the morning. She saw Steve's eyebrows lift a fraction at Price's peremptory remark but Price seemed not to notice.

He continued speaking, edging her closer to him. "She'll take a white wine, Blaylock. Riesling, if they have it. Will that suit?" Price questioned, increasing the pressure on her arm when she attempted to pull back.

Mutely Lee nodded, wishing she could jam an ice cube down his throat. She was sure she would choke on the sour taste of fury that seemed to be filling her mouth. Price was taking over again, relegating her to the status of child. She kept her eyes on Steve's retreating back.

"Rennie . . . Gilbert." Price sounded out the name like a lesson. "I'm curious. How did you pick that name?" His words were measured, his voice oddly hoarse, but Lee wasn't fooled. She could hear the anger vibrating in the words.

Lee was sure he couldn't be any angrier than she was. She tried again to wrench her arm free and only succeeded in hurting herself further. "Let me go, you bastard!" she hissed.

She saw the arrested look on his face and knew she had surprised him. The look was gone in a second, to be replaced by the angry glitter. "Well, well, whatever happened to that expensive finishing school veneer?" he rasped.

"It would be a waste of time to be ladylike to you," Lee shot back, watching the muscle jump in his cheek.

"Answer my question."

"Still the same Price. You bark and everybody jumps." Lee stepped back as violence wreathed his face. "All right." Lee took a deep breath, shifting her eyes from his face to his tie clip, then to his right hand. He was rolling an unlit pencil-slim cigar between thumb and forefinger. "Rennie comes from the last part of my first name, LaReine. Gilbert was my mother's maiden name." She lifted her chin still higher, facing that green marble chip stare.

"Gilbert? I never knew your mother's maiden name. I'm sure if Frederick knew it, he's forgotten it." At Lee's light shrug, that harsh look came into his face again, but before he could continue speaking he was seized by a spasm of coughing that made Lee frown. He forestalled her interruption by a wave of his hand. "We tried to find you. Why couldn't you face me? Why the coward's way? I could kill you for what you put us through. Frederick was torn apart by your disappearance . . ." Price coughed again. "I combed London and New York. You asked me not to put anyone on your trail, so like a fool I didn't . . . at first. By the time detectives were on it, you were hidden well." Price finished on a dry cough. Then he snatched the watery highball from her hand and swallowed the contents at a gulp.

"I'm sorry about Frederick . . ." Lee began.

"Sorry?" Price's voice had risen. Several persons near them turned inquiringly. "Sorry, the lady says." His voice lowered and he pulled her toward a vacant corner. "Hell, that's a milksop answer for what you put us through. You bitch. My father . . ." Price grated.

"Whatever you believe of me . . ." Lee interrupted, feeling her color heighten, "I love Frederick . . ."

"Love? You? I doubt that emotion could ever touch you . . ." Again Price was taken with a fit of coughing.

For a moment Lee forgot her anger. "Have you a cold, Price?"

His smile didn't mask his anger when he responded. "What the hell has that to do with anything? Yes, I have a cold. Why didn't you at least keep in contact with Frederick? That hurt him . . ."

Lee flinched, feeling guilty as she thought of the kindly man who had been a surrogate father to her. How could she explain to Price her need to get away and hide? She looked up at him again, for the first time noting the unhealthy flush on his cheeks, the too-bright eyes.

Before she could comment, Price gripped her arm again. "We have to talk, Lee . . ."

At that moment, Steve returned to them. "Sorry I took so long. Too much visiting along the way."

Lee smiled in relief. She wasn't getting anywhere talking to Price like this. She lifted the glass of white wine to her lips and thought she would call him at the Chatham apartment here in New York tomorrow. Perhaps they would both be more able to converse without hitting out at each other. She saw Steve's narrow-eyed look as Price removed his hand from her arm to take his drink.

At that moment Alma swooped down upon them, the well-endowed Darvi Lindquist in tow, her sharp eyes missing nothing. "Rennie, I don't think you've met Darvi . . ." Without pausing she turned to a frowning Price. "You told me you wanted to speak to Carter Dasson. He's here now," Alma stated, taking Price's arm and apologizing to Lee at the same time. She mumbled something about Steve taking care of Darvi. With her cigaretted holder clamped in her teeth, she bore Price away.

Darvi gave both Lee and Steve a blank look. Then without a word, she turned to follow Price.

Price must be really feeling feverish, Lee thought angrily, if he would let Alma take him in tow like that. Ordinarily he wouldn't allow it, Lee was sure. She remembered with shivering clarity how summarily he dealt with those who annoyed him. Lee tried not to watch as the swaying Darvi latched herself to Price again, furious that he didn't even try to push the woman away. *Could he be ill? Was that why he was so docile? No, that was silly,* Lee argued to herself.

Steve touched her arm. "Hey, I'm still here. Don't look so put out. The luscious Darvi treats everyone like that unless she wants to use them. The nicely veneered guttersnipe is the queen of the soaps." He turned her to face him squarely. "What would you say to a little more mixing, then leaving here and going to a nice little French place I know? The bouillabaisse is terrific. Do you like bouillabaisse?"

Lee looked at him, her smile strained. "Yes. Yes, as a matter of fact, I love it. Do you think we might leave now? I . . . I'll call Alma tomorrow and explain." Lee was gratified when Steve agreed at once. They decided to meet at the front entrance after Lee retrieved her wrap. All the way to the door she had the feeling that Price's hand would descend on her at any moment.

It seemed to take forever for the elevator to arrive, then take them to the street floor. She felt as though the lobby would never be crossed, that the taxi would never come. Lee breathed a sigh of relief as she sank back against the upholstery of the cab.

She never remembered giving her order when she and Steve reached the tiny French restaurant.

"Hey, come back, will you? What's troubling you, Rennie?" Steve quizzed, a puzzled smile on his face.

"What? Oh, I'm sorry. It's nothing, really. You were right, Steve. The food is excellent," Lee responded, knowing she could not discuss Price with him.

"Now, lady, don't try to do a job on me. You weren't thinking about the food when you were off in that dream world." Steve grinned ruefully. "And I know it isn't my dynamite personality . . . so . . . if you need a broad shoulder, I'm volunteering."

Lee nodded, swallowing a mouthful of bouillabaisse too quickly and coughing. When she could speak again, she disclaimed any problem but she knew by the narrow look he gave her that he wasn't buying her story.

"Do you have to leave tomorrow, Rennie? I would love to show you my New York." Steve mentioned several places, changing the subject, much to Lee's relief.

"Yes, I really must leave. I do my best writing at home and I'm behind on my latest work. Writer's block, I guess." She laughed, wondering what Steve would say if she told him the reason that she hadn't been writing for the past two weeks was because thoughts of her husband filled her mind to the exclusion of everything else.

Steve insisted that she take his business card so that she could call him when she was in New York again. When he returned her to the hotel, she was more relaxed than she had been all day.

As she settled into bed, she hoped her mellow mood would help her blot out memories that threatened to crowd her mind. She thumped her pillow hard, angry at herself. "Remember the bad things, you fool," she muttered into a now shapeless pillow.

Instead, she thought of his loving, his gentle persuasive hands and body on their special wedding night. She had been most apprehensive about the pain she had heard so much about. It still made her hot all over to remember her own delighted moans as Price made her vitally aware of her body and his. What a beautiful week they had had together in the south of France after their marriage. She could still recall how gentle he had been when she had sudden, grieving thoughts of her father. She relived her shyness when Price suggested that they swim in the nude off their own secluded beach, the wild tenderness of their lovemaking on the coarse sand after the swim. *My God,* Lee thought, her body tingling, *I really thought I had heaven on earth.* It was almost three o'clock in the morning when she fell into a fitful sleep.

The ringing of the telephone was a rude awakening. Lee hadn't left a wake-up call, she was sure. Groggily she blinked at her watch as she lifted the receiver. Eight o'clock. "What . . . what is it?" She swallowed at the dryness in her throat.

"Lee, Lee, wake up. It's Alma. I just had a call from Nick Petrus, Price's secretary. Lee, are you listening?" Alma rasped, her tones a little shrill.

"Yes, yes, Alma, I'm listening," Lee faltered, struggling into a sitting position.

"Price is in the hospital. Nick says the doctor diagnosed pneumonia. Lee?"

The room started to spin. Lee pictured Price's feverish-looking face at Alma's party. *I should have made him go home, get to bed at once,* she fretted to herself. *But how could I? I don't have the right anymore.* "Yes, yes, Alma. I'll get right to the hospital. Well . . . I'm not sure I can sign for his medical treatments. I'm not sure we're still married."

"Petrus is pretty sure you are," Alma interrupted brusquely. "I'll meet you at the hospital, Lee." Alma rang off.

Lee never remembered donning the two-piece black tweed suit in lightweight cotton, or making up, but the mirror told her as she was going out the door that she would pass muster.

The taxi ride was the usual one for Manhattan—wild, dangerous, crazy. Today it suited Lee's mood.

At the hospital reception desk, Lee cleared her throat for attention. Before she could respond to the questioning look of the nurse, a hand at her elbow turned her away.

"Mrs. Chatham, I'm Nick Petrus. I don't think we've ever met. I've only been with your husband for two years." The suavely handsome slim-built Greek smiled into her eyes.

Lee smiled back, instinctively liking him, noting the slight hesitation in his voice at the word "husband."

"Are you not sure that my husband and I are married, Mr. Petrus?" Lee quizzed him, her tones crisp.

Unembarrassed, he tilted his head, as though acknowledging her correct assessment of his thoughts. "I know that your husband has not divorced you . . . but . . ." His shrug was totally Grecian, his white teeth setting off his olive skin when he smiled at her.

"I have not divorced my husband," Lee whispered, wondering why she should feel such a surge of relief when Nick told her that Price had not divorced her.

With a satisfied smile Petrus led her toward a closed door. Lee held back, her throat dry. "Is this Price's room?"

"No, Mrs. Chatham, this is Dr. Clermont's office. It won't take a minute to sign the papers, then you can see your husband."

Lee tried to smother the warm glow spreading through her as she signed the papers for his treatment. Price hadn't divorced her. She looked up to listen to a young, very sharp-minded doctor speaking concisely to her. Lee questioned him closely for several moments before she was satisfied Price would get the best care.

"Thank you, Mrs. Chatham. Now you would like to see your husband, I'm sure. Nurse Pelham tells me that a Miss Lindquist is with him at the moment but I'm sure that you can go right along to his room."

Lee felt as though she had been dipped in dry ice, the coldness penetrating to her soul. Nothing had changed. "Ah, Doctor Clermont, I think I'll not wait. Mr. Petrus, will you take these flowers to Mr. Chatham. Thank you." Lee thrust the violets she had purchased from the vendor in front of the hospital at the bewildered secretary. She ignored the open-mouthed stares of the two men, almost running from the room toward the elevator.

When the elevator doors opened, Lee walked straight into Alma, who snatched at her arm, holding her back.

"Where are you going, Lee? Have you seen Price? Is he all right?" Alma rapidly fired the questions at her.

Lee took a deep shuddering breath, trying to school her features so that Alma wouldn't see the pain she was trying to hide. "No, Alma, I haven't seen Price, but . . . but I have talked to the doctor. All the steps have been taken to insure that Price will have the best of care. Pardon me, I have to leave."

"Lee, what in hell is the matter? What's going on? God, you can't just pop off like a rabbit and not have me wonder," Alma sputtered.

"I'm sorry, Alma. I don't want to talk about it. Give my regards to Price. I'll leave my address with your office. I . . . just . . . can't . . . stay," Lee grated, swallowing hard. She thumbed the elevator button until her hand hurt.

Alma squeezed Lee's shoulder. "Call me when you reach home. Perhaps we can talk again. Remember that you're dear to me, Lee."

Lee planted a quick kiss on Alma's cheek before the elevator whisked her to the lobby.

* * *

The return plane trip didn't hold her interest. The spreading hands of the Finger Lakes did not give the familiar touch of pleasure. She barely remembered claiming her car and driving the hour-long trip to Highland Farms. She felt bone-weary and drained.

Nothing seemed to go right when she got home. Rica stubbornly refused to go to bed at the usual time and Lee had to be sharp with her. She also knew that Gladdy was watching her closely. Finally, after three bedtime stories, Rica settled down.

When she joined Gladdy in the lounge, Lee went at once to the large window wall and threw back the drapes. The lake glinted like silver in the star-dappled night. The air was like new wine, too sharp, too fresh.

"Lee." Gladdy cleared her throat, noticing Lee's startled movement, her fingers clenching on the drapes. "Sorry, Lee, I didn't mean to spook you." She cleared her throat once more. "It doesn't take a mind reader to figure that you haven't settled anything with Price Chatham. Did you see him at all?"

"Yes. Yes, Gladdy, I saw him. We didn't have much chance to talk. He's in the hospital . . . pneumonia. It's all right. He doesn't need me. A woman by the name of Darvi Lindquist is with him, caring for him."

"Darvi Lindquist? The Darvi Lindquist who is on my soap opera?" Gladdy said, open-mouthed with surprise.

"What? Soap opera? It could be. Yes. Someone said that she was on TV," Lee said, keeping her voice level with great effort. "I know that she's quite beautiful. I signed some release forms for his treatment. Price doesn't need me for anything else." Lee's voice cracked. She bit down on her lower lip.

"Lee, for corn's sake, why didn't you just tell her to get the hell out of there? You're Price's wife. I don't understand you. You make business decisions every day, with your writing, with the farm, yet with your own husband you have this terrible blind spot. Lee . . ."

Lee turned slowly away from the sliding glass doors, her right hand held palm outward, toward Gladdy. "No. No more. I don't want to talk about Price anymore. Tomorrow evening Grant will be coming over. I'm going to tell him to begin divorce proceedings. He can do it any way he chooses, as long as it gets done fast. Good night, Gladdy."

Sleep didn't come to her easily that night or many of the following nights, but Lee was able to fill her days with intense concentration on her new book. She dined with Grant several times, some nights at the club, others in the rather good restaurants in the surrounding area. Despite feeling uncomfortable with Grant's family, she dined with him at his sister's home one evening. Lee found Tansy Culver, Grant's sister, and her husband, Phil, to be pompous in the extreme.

"Lee, do you buy all of your clothes in New York?"

Lee set her delicate china coffee cup on the low table in front of the settee before answering her hostess. "Not all of them, Tansy, but I do like to shop in New York. I love the choice and the styles."

"But, don't you see," Tansy interjected smoothly, "that's the problem. You look a trifle outlandish here in our community, with those New York styles. Perhaps if you were taller"—she smiled at Lee deprecatingly—"you would have more panache."

Lee allowed her eyes to widen, her brows lifting slowly, as her gaze roved over Tansy from head to foot. "Panache, did you say, Tansy?"

A mottled red stained Tansy's cheeks. Before she could retort, Lee rose and stepped to Grant's side, telling him she was tired and wished to leave.

"That was a nice evening, wasn't it, Lee?" Grant said firmly.

Lee looked out the window of the car, at the lake glistening in the soft moonlight, as they climbed the curving road. "Was it, Grant? To be accurate, I find your sister heavy going."

Grant's head swiveled toward her. Lee knew without looking that he would be frowning.

"Now, Lee honey, you mustn't mind anything Tansy says. She's direct, I know, but she's quite a social leader here in . . ."

"Please, Grant, spare me. Your sister quoted chapter and verse on her many social accomplishments. I'd rather not hear any more," Lee interrupted, her voice laced with irritation.

The silence stretched right through their tense good nights. Lee felt only relief as she shut the door and went to bed.

Two weeks after her return from New York, Lee began to feel that she was really making headway on the new book. She had almost succeeded in shutting out everything and everyone but Rica and Gladdy from her thoughts. The concentration was having good results.

When Gladdy buzzed through that she was wanted on the phone, one early afternoon, she swallowed her irritation at the interruption. Dr. Spellman wanted to speak with her, Gladdy said. Lee remembered how good he had been to her when she was having Rica as she lifted the phone and spoke. "Yes, Dr. Spellman? How are you? . . . What? Yes, my husband's name is Price Chatham . . . Yes, I'll be right there. It will take about forty-five minutes to an hour, depending on the traffic. Strong Memorial Hospital. Right. Good-bye." Lee huddled next to the phone for a moment, trying to still the tremors that shook her.

Rising from behind her desk, she went to the kitchen, blinking at Gladdy when the woman spoke to her.

"What's the matter, Lee? You're paper white."

Lee put both hands up to her face, almost as though she

were trying to squeeze blood back into it. "It's Price. He collapsed at the thruway exit at Victor. They've taken him to Strong Memorial. Doctor Spellman was there when they brought him in. He recognized the name. He called to see if it was any relation." Lee swallowed with difficulty. "God, Gladdy, I have to go right away. He must not have been fully recovered from the pneumonia. What was he doing at Victor?" Lee faltered. Her throat was so tight, it hurt.

Gladdy sighed. "I think we both know he was looking for you. Now, forget that for now. You go to the hospital and get him. Bring him back to Highlands. He can recuperate here. What could be nicer than the Bristols, with July coming on and the lake warming up," Gladdy said briskly, pushing Lee toward the hall leading to the bedrooms.

Lee found Gulick Road with its curving beauty far from appealing. She wanted to shout at the dawdling cars in front of her. Passing was well nigh impossible most of the way. By the time she reached the hospital in Rochester, her nerves were ragged.

Dr. Spellman met her near the Emergency entrance. "Now, Lee, don't look so worried. He's all right, just worn out. I understand that he's had a bout of pneumonia. What's the matter with people? Why can't they take that disease seriously?"

Lee didn't look at Dr. Spellman once as they walked down the hall but she was very aware of his narrow-eyed glances. He stopped in front of a closed door, putting a hand on her arm. "Lee, I'll tell you straight. He can leave here today . . . but . . . he has to have somewhere to rest. I would rather he wasn't at a motel . . . Now, I don't know what kind of relationship you have with your husband . . ."

"It's all right, Doctor Spellman, I'm taking him home with me. Thank you for all you've done. Is this my husband's room?" Lee queried, still avoiding the doctor's looks.

Dr. Spellman nodded, pushing the door open. Lee looked past him into the room. Price seemed to be sleeping but he opened his eyes almost at once, looking right into hers. Lee barely listened to the doctor's terse remarks before he left the room.

"I'm taking you home with me, Price. I've already arranged for your rented car to be picked up . . ." Lee said curtly, her voice fading as she took note of Price's pale face, fatigue lines grooving from his eyes to his mouth. "You should never have attempted such a trip when you'd just come out of the hospital. Do you think you are able to travel home today?"

"Yes." His voice was harsh but Lee thought it had lost some of the hoarseness that she had noticed at Alma's party. His eyes, which had never left her, were burning cold and hard.

Lee gazed around the room, wishing Price would stop staring at her. She was determined that he wouldn't disconcert her but she was not as steady as she would have liked. She cleared her throat. "Would you like me to help you . . . that is . . . ah . . . can you dress yourself?"

"Why? Would you dress me if I needed it, Lee?" Price grated, a contemptuous curl to his pallid lips.

Lee reddened, angry with herself and angry with him for making her feel so defensive. She looked down at her stiff fingers plucking at the bedcovers. "Yes, I would help you, if you needed it. I would help any ill person. Do you need help?"

"No, however tempting it might be." Price's sardonic smile chipped away at her, chilling her. As she turned toward the door, his voice stopped her. "Are you going to run out on me again, Lee?" he asked with a snarl in his voice.

Without looking around at him, one hand on the door handle, she shook her head no.

Lee was grateful for the cup of coffee one of the nurses brought to her, but before it was half gone, Price was beside her, an overnight case in one hand. Lee reached for the case but Price shook his head. They both said their good-byes to Dr. Spellman and listened to his instructions for Price, which seemed to consist mostly of rest and relaxation.

Lee was glad the highway was busy on the return trip. Conversation was in limbo while she fought the traffic.

"You drive well, Lee. I don't think I've ever ridden with you before, have I?" Price queried, his tone indifferent, as though he were making polite conversation with a stranger. He had turned slightly in his seat to watch her.

"Of course not," Lee responded tartly, "you would never let a mere woman drive you. Not the great Price Chatham, heaven forbid!"

Price gave a mirthless laugh. "Come off it, Lee. What ever gave you the idea that I was like that? I've never felt threatened by a woman's accomplishments. I don't think I ever showed that I wasn't proud of you. I was always that. We weren't married long enough for either of us to get to know the other properly but I can assure you I would have been most interested in anything you wanted to try. Any field of endeavor that you wished for would not have been closed to you. I wasn't married to you long enough to know your dreams."

"You considered me a baby," Lee said bitchily. "Babies don't have dreams or talents outside of being decorative and amusing."

"Well, you couldn't be described as that anymore, could you?" Price quizzed, his tones silky.

Lee wasn't fooled. She knew if she looked at him, his eyes would be rock hard. She refused to accept that his words hurt her and lashed back at him. "No, I couldn't and don't you forget it, Price Chatham."

"Cool down, you little devil. Where the hell did that

temper come from? You were such a sweet little thing . . ." Price began.

"Sweet little thing! Thing! That's the operative word. I was just a possession to you. Something you took out now and then to stroke for a while then put away," Lee blurted, wishing she could stop the flow of words out of her mouth. She felt like a dam that had bust.

"I thought you liked the stroking as much as I did, darling," Price growled softly, real amusement in his voice.

"Why you . . . you . . ." Lee sputtered, her eyes leaving the road for a moment to glare at Price.

He straightened from his lounging position as horns blared, and Lee had to turn fast, almost overcorrecting them into the drainage ditch at the side of the road. "All right, Lee. We either table the discussion or you calm down. Obviously we differ on . . ."

"You're right there. We differ on almost everything," she answered stiffly, her hands at eleven and one o'clock on the wheel.

"Lee, I was always aware of the difference in our age and attitude. Naturally, I should think," he snapped, settling back against the seat.

"Naturally," Lee said sarcastically. "You can bet your boots our attitudes were different on *many* things . . ." Her tones were waspish but she couldn't seem to help herself. Why could she never be cool with him?

Price turned sideways on the seat, one hand coming out to clench her shoulder. "Say it, Lee. Say what's bothering you. Felice Harvey," he snapped. "Don't go all white on me. It didn't take a Sherlock Holmes to figure it out. Scylla was only too happy to inform me that you had been to town, that she had assumed you had stayed at the flat. You came in when Felice was there, didn't you?" His voice was hard without a tinge of remorse, it seemed to Lee. "You ran when you discovered that Darvi was in my hospital room, didn't you?"

"Damn you, I didn't run from the hospital room. I'm not the same blind, besotted girl you married, Price," Lee shot back. "I *left* the hospital because I refuse to become a witness to a cloying reuinion between you and one of your harem mates."

"You bitch. Where the hell do you get off judging anyone after the vanishing act you pulled throwing Frederick's and my life into turmoil. . . . Oh, the hell with it . . ." Price muttered a harsh expletive and sank back against the seat back, closing his eyes.

With a guilty start, Lee realized how much their arguing was taxing him. "I told you that I was sorry about Frederick, Price." She spoke in measured tones, throwing quick glances his way.

"Do you know what he said when I called him from the hospital to say that I had found you?" Price quizzed her, his eyes still closed. "He said tell Lee that I love her and want her to come home to Stone Manor."

Lee swallowed a sob, wishing with all her heart that she could take Rica and go to the man who was holding out his fatherly arms to her. She promised herself that she would see Frederick soon.

When the silence stretched between them, Lee glanced over at Price, wincing a little at his pallor, and realized he had fallen asleep. She sighed, gripping the wheel, aware that her palms were moist.

All at once his head slid sideways on the seat back, coming to rest on her shoulder. She didn't try to question the spread of warmth that went through her at his nearness. She bit her lip hard as she told herself to stay armed against him. She tried to stay very still so that she wouldn't disturb him.

They were a few miles from Highland Farms when Price wakened. Lee knew it when she felt his hand come across her middle, pressing gently.

"I remember sleeping on your shoulder, wife. Perhaps my head was a little lower than that," he drawled.

Lee fought the blush that she could feel staining her face. "As long you are awake you may as well sit up. I would give any sick person the usage of my shoulder," she said stiffly.

His hand tightened on her hip bone in a painful grip.

"There's Highland Farms Road," she gasped. "There, now you can see the house. It's really quite beautiful up here in the hills."

"Yes, isn't it," Price said harshly, pulling his hand from her hip. "Easy does it turning that wheel. That drainage ditch looks deep."

"It is," Lee grated, *and maybe if you left me alone I could have driven better,* she thought angrily.

All other thoughts were driven from her mind as she saw Rica on the sloping lawn area leading from the house to the road. The child was standing next to Gladdy, holding her hand, jumping up and down in her excitement.

"God, Lee, the place is quite beautiful, sitting on top of the hill like that. What a view of the lake you must have!" Price said, speaking casually. Lee felt a sudden change in him, the stiffening as he straightened in his seat. She jumped at his next words. "Who the hell is that? That child . . . does she belong to that woman?"

Lee didn't answer as she eased the car up the grade toward the garage. She pulled the emergency brake on and stopped from the car to embrace the bouncing little girl. It seemed to Lee that Rica's childish voice was trumpet loud.

"Is he my daddy, Mommy? Is he? Gladdy says you brung him. Did you?" Not waiting for an answer Rica pushed herself away from Lee and looked solemnly up at a white, frozen-faced Price. "Are you my daddy? I fell off my swing but I didn't cry." Rica's curls, black and so like Price's, bobbed as she moved.

Lee watched Price swallow, his eyes fixed on the child looking up at him. He dropped to one knee, curling his hand around Rica's pointing finger. His voice was tight and low. "Yes. I'm your daddy," Price said huskily. "Your coloring is like your grandmother Chatham but your smile is like . . . someone else's. What's your name, love?"

"Rica . . . Fred-da-rica." Rica beamed toothily at her father, their rapport instant and total.

Price rose to his feet. Lee could feel his rapier stare as she bent to kiss her daughter. She could think of nothing to say. To her relief Gladdy stepped forward.

"I'm Gladys Ogilvie, but everyone calls me Gladdy. I was a close friend of Lee's mother . . . and . . . I'm a close friend of Lee's," the housekeeper said, her eyes glinting in a martial light.

Price took the proffered hand, the mocking smile momentarily softening the tough glacial lines of his jaw. "How do you do, Gladdy. I'm Lee's husband. Now just where does that put us?"

Gladdy frowned for a moment, studying him, then shrugged, not moving from Lee's side.

Rica, who had been trying to wrestle a red ball from the mouth of the Labrador, Duke, finally succeeded. The dog panted, staying close to Rica, watching both the child and the ball. Rica pulled at Price's jacket. "This is Duke. He's my dog. Do you like him?"

"Very much." Price smiled as he leaned over Rica again, the sudden dimples at the side of his mouth making Lee catch her breath. She felt a sudden resentment that even ill he could still look vitally handsome, dynamic.

"What do I call you? Uncle Price like Uncle Grant?" Rica frowned.

Price straightened, turning a burning glance at Lee, then he looked back at the child, the smile touching his mouth again. "You can call me Daddy, Rica. Would you like that?"

Rica tilted her head sideways, one chubby hand on her cheek, a pensive look on her face. Neither Price nor Lee moved. Then Rica smiled, nodding her head, gamboling away with the dog.

"She's like you, Lee." Price's voice was clipped.

"No. No, Price, she isn't." Lee said unsteadily. "She's like you, the green eyes, the black curly hair . . ."

"Not her looks, Lee, her mannerisms, that way of holding her head," Price said harshly.

Gladdy cleared her throat. "That's what I say too, Mr. Chatham. She's so like Lee at this age. Now, enough of this. You've been ill, I hear," Gladdy said briskly. "You had better come along with me. No, don't bother with your case. I'll have Tom bring it. Lunch is on the patio."

There was a minor crisis when Lee asked Rica to put her tricycle away before lunch. When Rica turned mulish, Price, with smooth firmness, turned the rebellion into acquiescence. When she noticed the pinched look around Price's mouth, Lee stifled a prickle of resentment.

"Would you like your lunch in bed, Price?" Lee asked.

"No. I'll eat on the patio, then I'll lie down for a while." He bit the words out, not looking at her. "It's beautiful here. A little like being on top of the world." His tones were offhand but Lee could sense his rage.

Rica dominated the lunch and took all Price's attention, much to Lee's relief. Rica was ecstatic when Price fed the tail-wagging Duke from the table. Neither Lee nor Gladdy said a word.

When Gladdy rose from the table to take Rica in for a nap, Lee stood as well, beginning to clear the table. Price's hand closed on her arm. "Leave it, Lee. You can show me to my room first." Price's eyes were emerald hard. Lee couldn't shake off his arm. He rose from his chair, not releasing her, motioning her forward.

Resentment and a niggling fear battled within her. How she hated this man who seemed to think he could control even her movements. Not able to free herself from his manacle hold, she turned, stiff with anger, to lead him to his room.

"The house is unusual, and it doesn't look that old," Price remarked, looking at the Spanish tile walls and floor in the corridor leading to the sleeping area.

At first Lee was not going to respond but the love and pride she had in the house her father had built for her mother won over the anger she felt toward Price. "The house, as you might have noticed, is like an abstract letter H." She cleared her throat, not liking to be this close to him. "Rica and I sleep in the wing on the lake side. The kitchen and dining area are on the matching wing on the other side of the house. You will be across the courtyard from Rica and me . . . in the guest wing. Here we are." Lee pointed out the sliding glass door that led to a flagstone patio between the wings. "See, because the wings are cocked at an angle you will have a view of the lake as well even though you are on the road side of the house. Do you like it?"

"Very much. Does that sliding glass door opposite lead to your room?" Price asked, his eyes hooded.

"Yes," Lee said, angry that she could feel her face flushing.

"You should blush. With shame," he said curtly, reaching out and slamming the door to the bedroom shut. "At last a little privacy to tell you what I think of you . . . but there aren't words strong enough to describe you, you bitch. Why the hell didn't you tell me we had a child? What is the matter with you? Anyone can see that Rica is mine," he erupted, starting for her.

"No," Lee flared, putting a hand flat on his chest, checking him. "No, Rica is mine. Mine. I want a divorce, Price. I'm going to marry again . . ."

"Are you?" he asked. "Don't tell me. Let me guess who it must be . . . Uncle Grant," he said sardonically. "Well we'll see . . . we'll see." He grasped her upper arms, making her wince. Sweat beaded his upper lip as he struggled with the violence that was coursing through him.

Lee saw the grayish cast to his skin. "Price, Price, please

let me go. You're not well. Please. We'll talk another time. There's the door to your bathroom. Get your pajamas on. I'll wait here." She was almost pleading with him. The putty-colored look of his skin frightened her.

He thrust her away from him, making her stumble. Lee didn't exhale until she heard the water running in the bathroom.

By the time Price was in bed he was exhausted. Lee hovered over him, not sure if she should stay.

His right arm shot out, shackling her wrist, surprising her with his strength as he pulled her to a sitting position next to him on the bed. "Lee, tell me. You must have had her not too long after you left me."

"A little over six months. I . . . I didn't know I was pregnant until I was here at the farm," Lee whispered, looking down at the hand that imprisoned her.

"You should have let me know. I had a right to know," he rasped. Then he sighed tiredly. "Did you have rough time, Lee?"

"It was rough." Lee smiled a tight smile. "The doctor said I should not plan on too many babies . . . I'm too narrow-hipped." She was sorry the moment she spoke, not wanting to put the conversation on such a personal level. She bit her lip, trying not to look away when his eyes moved over her.

"You were always small—not everywhere, of course," he said absently. He released her wrist, letting his right index finger touch the cleavage of the cotton blouse she was wearing.

Lee cursed the blush she knew was reddening her skin and pulled back, her mouth tight.

Price's eyebrows rose, taking malicious note of her discomfort. "Still blushing like an innocent? Too bad I know better, isn't it? Too bad I know you're a hard, vindictive woman of twenty-six wearing the mask of a sweet girl. Right?" He bit the words out, the muscle working in his cheek. He tried to take hold of her arm again but she broke free, jumping to her feet, her hands clenched.

"And you're the same bastard you've always been. It's soothing to know that there's one constant in this world. That Price Chatham was, is, and will be an unmitigated bastard . . . at the grand old age of thirty-eight," Lee burst out chokingly, forgetting all her self-made promises about being calm in front of Price. A red haze seemed to cover her eyes. She whirled away to the door.

His voice, abrasive as flint, stopped her in the doorway. "Rica is mine too, Lee. I'm staying here . . . staying. And nothing or no one will drive me away."

CHAPTER THREE

The temperature hovered at ninety degrees in July. The earth sweltered in the piercing sunlight. Swimming was more important than eating. Even sitting high on the hill it was sometimes impossible to catch a breeze in the late afternoon. Sailing was done in the early morning. It seemed as though Price had been at Highland Farms forever even though it had been just three weeks. His weakness had disappeared entirely and he seemed to have no bad aftereffects. He and Rica were inseparable.

Grant Lieber was visibly irritated by his presence and often mentioned he thought it was time for Price to leave. "He looks well enough to me, Lee. It's not good for Rica to have him around this long. It will be harder for her to part with him later."

Lee sighed, nodding. "I know that . . . but . . . he's her father. Little girls love their father . . ."

"Exactly the point I'm making, Lee," Grant said in his most forceful courtroom manner. "All this nonsense must stop. It's not good for her to have all this spoiling; when she lives with us she will think that's the way a home should be. It's not. With us she'll get firm and loving discipline. That's what she needs."

Lee bent down to pull a dead leaf from one of the red geraniums that edged the patio. She didn't want Grant to see the confusion registering on her face. She crushed the dry leaf in her hand, smiling as she remembered Price and Rica planting them. What a mess they had made! It was going to be so painful for Rica when Price left. The thought made her wince. What was she to do? Rising, she turned to the frowning man at her side, trying to smile. "You're coming to dinner tonight, aren't you, Grant?"

"Of course. I come for dinner every Wednesday. I'll be here at seven," he remarked sententiously. "Have the steaks ready. I'll grill them as usual," Grant promised, leaving shortly afterward.

That evening, to Lee's irritation, Price seemed to have other ideas about the steaks. She had excused herself from the regular before-dinner swim with Rica because she felt she couldn't face Price without showing her anger. They had had words again about the custody of Rica and Price was being adamant in his refusal to leave her with Lee all the time. Instead she had taken a long, cold shower, trying to cool down her body and her temper. When she went out onto the patio she found him standing in front of the gas barbecue. He was moving his hand slowly over the heat as though to check its readiness. He turned at the sound of her heels on the stone and looked her over from head to toe and back again. "I think we have time for a drink, Lee, before I put the steaks on. Gladdy tells me everything else is ready," Price said curtly, his eyes never leaving her.

"Yes . . . well, there's no need for you to barbecue the steaks, Price." She spoke a little stiffly, she knew, but his piercing stare made her uncomfortable. "Grant always does them when he arrives. He should be here shortly."

Price was silent, his hot gaze still moving over her. Lee fought to keep from blushing. She ground her teeth in helpless rage as she felt the heat building in her. He did it on purpose, she fumed to herself.

"You have good taste, wife. The cheongsam suits you. Most Occidental women are too heavy-boned to wear them . . . but not you, my sweet." His voice had a sensuous overtone that made Lee uneasy. "My blond Oriental. That color suits you. What do you call it? Chinese blue?" he quizzed, one black eyebrow arched.

"Turquoise," Lee said, clenching her fists. "Price, about the steaks . . . Grant always . . ."

"Hmmmm, turquoise. Very nice with your eyes," he interrupted smoothly. "Don't worry about the steaks," he said, turning back to the grill. "Tonight they'll be the way I like them and the way you liked them years ago . . . medium rare, not done to shoe leather."

Lee's snapped her teeth together, frustration burning her at the easy way he assumed control in her house. As she searched for a remark cutting enough to pierce his armor, she again became aware of his assessing glance. She stamped her foot in desperation. "Stop looking at me like that," she fumed.

"Like what, wife?"

"And don't call me wife, either," Lee gasped. She wanted desperately to upend the charcoal scuttle over his head.

"You are my wife, Lee. Don't forget that. I don't," he said harshly. Before she divined his intention, he had crossed the space between them, grasping her wrist and pulling her off balance into his arms. She was fastened tight to him before she could do more than gasp. His mouth lowered. He didn't seem put out when she turned her face away. Instead he let his mouth feather down her cheek to her ear. "See how restrained I am with you, wife. I would really like to make a canapé out of your earlobe and munch away but I'm afraid that then I would want the main course," he whispered mockingly, running his tongue along the curve of her ear.

Breathless, Lee shivered, trying to pull away, but Price's arms tightened, holding her close to his length. Without thinking she rubbed her cheek against Price's lowered one. When she heard him chuckle she tried to wrench free without success.

"This is where you belong, Lee," he muttered, his hard kiss parting her lips, taking her breath, making the blood pound in her ears.

When he lifted his head she was reeling. She hardly

noticed the set look about his mouth when she was finally able to pull free. As she stood, taking deep breaths to steady herself, the white metal screen door slid back and Grant stepped in from the living room.

"Lee, dear, how nice you look." Grant sent a quick narrow-eyed look at Price before enfolding her in his arms and kissing her hard and long. Lee lay quiescent in his arms, trying not to show how nervous she was. Grant lifted his head from their kiss, but didn't release her. As he stared at Price, an angry curl came to his lips. "Chatham. You seem better, much better to me. Isn't it time you were back in New York or London or wherever it is you belong?"

Lee stiffened, trying to step away from him, wishing he hadn't confronted Price in such a fashion.

She watched Price warily. When he turned to face Grant, seemingly relaxed, a friendly expression on his face, she became even more vigilant.

"Are you so sure that I don't belong *here?*" Price's voice was smooth. "I'm in my wife's home, with my daughter. I think the outsider is you." His low tones hardened. "And, by the way, the next time you kiss my wife, make it a peck on the cheek. I'm the jealous type."

Grant almost flung Lee from his side, his cheeks a mottled red.

Price's stance didn't change. Instead he turned away, a wry twist to his lips, and looked at Lee. "Get the steaks now, will you? And call Rica. Have a drink, Lieber. You look as though you could use one." Price looked back at Grant, his whole demeanor a deliberate challenge.

Lee didn't wait to hear any more, glad of the chance to escape the heavy atmosphere.

The tray of steaks was sitting in the fridge next to a cut glass bowl of greens, ready to toss. Gladdy eyed Lee's flustered motions but didn't comment.

Lee didn't look at either man when she handed over the steaks to Price. She just swiveled away, mumbling something about getting Rica, furious with herself that she didn't tell Price to get the bloody hell away from the steaks and let the sulking Grant cook them.

Rica was hot, tired, and very dusty from playing games with Duke and her friend Johnny Greenway, who lived on the other side of the mountain. Johnny's father raised and sold quarterhorses with limited success. He often helped in the vineyards to supplement his income. Lee considered the Greenways good friends and good neighbors.

"Can Johnny stay and have steak with us, Mommy?" Rica asked, slapping her hands down her jeans, making a miniature dust storm. Without waiting for her mother's answer she turned to her friend. "Do you like steak, Johnny?"

The tow-headed boy, as grubby as Rica, screwed up his face. "I dunno . . . maybe . . ."

Lee took a deep breath, deciding not to wait for the debate on whether Johnny would like steaks. "Johnny, why don't you stay? I'll call your mother. Then later, I'll walk you down the hill and through the vineyard when it's time to go home."

"Okay," he said, with relief that he didn't have to make the decision.

Lee spearheaded the dawdling children right to the laundry room shower that opened off the side yard. She prayed she could find some zipper-front jeans and an old shirt of Rica's that would fit Johnny. No doubt she would have to pin them on him because Rica's frame was chubbier. She tried to keep a smile on her face even though she was grinding her teeth at the thought of what Price might be saying to Grant.

With Gladdy's help the two children were scrubbed and presented at the table in record time. Price's raised eyebrow acknowledged her flush cheeks and her hair in slight disarray. Grant frowned at Lee, then looked at the children.

Rica intervened, taking Grant's hand. "Hi, Uncle Grant. Do you know my friend, Johnny?"

"Yes, I do. Give me a kiss, Rica," Grant demanded, lifting the child in his arms, looking at Price in triumph. When he set Rica back on her feet, he looked at Johnny, watching them in grave interest. "How are you, boy? Is your father still out of work? I hear tell they're hiring at Mobil . . ."

Lee winced, wishing Grant wouldn't talk so bluntly in front of the children. After all, it was no one's business what the Greenways financial picture was, she thought. She watched Johnny, hoping he wouldn't be discomfited.

Johnny looked at Grant for long moments, his basset hound eyes intent. "My daddy isn't out of work. We have horses. Are you out of work, Mr. Lieber? Should I ask my daddy if you can help with the horses? He'll let you, I think, unless you're cow handed. Are you?"

Price's bark of laughter made both Rica and Johnny jump. Then they both smiled at him, not sure what had made him so mirthful. He cupped his hands around the backs of their heads and drew them toward him. "Come over here with me, you two, and help me cook these steaks. Help yourself to one of those glasses of lemonade and tell me what you have been doing all day."

"I swam with you, Daddy. Did you forget?" Rica looked at him, puzzled.

"No, angel, I didn't forget . . ." Price smiled down at them.

Lee turned away, faintly irritated that she had not been included in the conversation. She started when Grant took hold of her arm.

"Lee, I insist he must go. Tansy was just saying how the gossip is increasing about you . . . about him being here," he said heavily.

"Grant." Lee took a deep breath. "I don't like gossip and I don't like gossipers . . . but I can't see the wrong in Price being at this house. Now, don't look so angry. I don't want him here. Hopefully he'll be leaving soon . . . but I'm sure he will be coming back many times. Rica is his daughter and he is determined to keep it that way. I can't deny him visitation rights."

"No, perhaps not, but we'll work out something less awkward than this after we're married. I'll see to it," Grant said firmly.

"Let's eat, shall we?" Lee said, sighing.

Lee found the steaks excellent and avoided Grant's censuring stare as much as possible.

Grant's irritation extended to the children, and he found fault with them at every turn.

Once stirred up the overtired children became fractious. Lee felt only relief when Grant left early. She didn't even try to soothe his ruffled feathers. She could hardly wait to get Rica to bed, very grateful when Price offered to walk Johnny down the hill. She walked into the kitchen, looking at Gladdy tiredly. "There, she's settled for the night." She looked around the kitchen. "Why not leave the rest of this until morning?"

"Suits me. What an awful evening. I've never seen those two children so edgy. Where are you off to now, Lee?" Gladdy quizzed.

"I think I'll take a swim before I go to bed. It's so warm and I feel sticky and strung up. Good night, Gladdy."

Not wanting to face Price, Lee scrambled into her suit and hustled out the door to the road leading to the beach. It was a bit of a hike down the winding road but Lee welcomed the exercise. The stars were so clear she didn't even use the flashlight she was carrying. The whining snuffles at her left side told her that Duke had decided to accompany her. "No skinny dipping tonight, Duke old boy," Lee whispered, laughing, to the dog. "With that streetlamp moon and stars, it's like daylight."

The only sounds on the beach were the lapping of the wavelets on the shore and the bright *chreeps* of the crickets. There was almost no breeze as she walked out to the end of the stone jetty. Instead of diving from the end, Lee lowered herself down the wooden ladder into the water. It was cool but not cold. She gasped a satisfied breath and stroked outward toward the wooden float anchored in deeper water. She swam around the raft then downward toward an unused section of beach. She was vaguely aware that Duke was swimming somewhere near her. His contented snuffles were another soothing night sound.

She was swimming back toward the float when she noticed an arrow of rippled water in deeper water, out farther. Duke was on the land side of her and didn't seem apprehensive, but Lee was uneasy. What was making that wake? It disappeared. Then something touched her. Momentary panic made her swallow water.

"Easy, Lee, it's just me. You shouldn't be swimming alone at night, even if Duke is with you." Price breathed next to her, moving easily. "I must say it was a good idea, though. It's a beautiful night."

"You frightened me." Lee coughed, splashing water at him. She saw the sudden glint in his eye and flipped sideways trying to stroke away. She felt an iron hand clasp her ankle and pull her back. Laughing, she fought him, trying to get both hands on his head to duck him. It gave her gleeful satisfaction as she felt his head sink into the water. She pressed harder. Then she realized that he had taken an iron hold on her middle and was taking her down with him. She barely managed to gulp a breath before she was beneath the surface. She pulled on his hair hoping to make him free her but it just brought his head level with hers. He clamped his mouth to hers. They broke water with Lee struggling to free herself. She was breathless, her heart thudding painfully when he released her, her reactions to his kiss confusing her. She ground her teeth together as she stroked hard for the jetty. Damn him to hell! He had always been able to draw a response from her. Damn all physical attraction! That's all it was. That's all it had ever been to Price! She was older now, not the dumb twenty-year-old who thought he was the moon and the stars. She reached the ladder, but before she could pull herself up Price had circled her waist with one arm, bringing her back against him so that her head was almost on his shoulder.

"Do you remember the night we swam in the sea on our honeymoon, Lee? The only covering you had on your body was my arms." Price's voice was silky soft.

Water splashed into Lee's mouth as she tried to free herself. "No, I don't remember. I'm not interested in ancient history," Lee snapped, a sudden shiver coursing her body.

"Liar." Price laughed harshly, lifting her body up the ladder.

Lee felt him stroke her leg and cursed the weakness she felt.

Before she could lift her towel, Price was there, shooing away a dripping Duke, who was intent on shaking water on them. Price wrapped her in the towel, slowly rubbing her dry. "Come along to the beach. I'll light a fire. I have a bottle of Highland Farms champagne in the jeep. I'll get it."

A shivering Lee watched him put a match to the pile of dry twigs, not looking directly at him. "I thought that I would just dry a little and go on up. You can come . . ."

"Forget that," Price interrupted harshly. "We'll have some wine and then go up together." He turned away abruptly and went over to the big storage shed and brought out some bath sheets. "Here, take off your bikini and wrap in this."

Lee rebelled for a moment but a sudden breeze sent a shudder through her and she grabbed at the towel ungraciously and went to the shed.

When she returned, Price was waiting, a glass of wine in his hand, which he extended toward her. He had a short toweling wrap around his waist. *He looks like a South Sea*

Islander, Lee thought giddily, knowing he had discarded his own swim briefs. "Come over here and sit by the fire and quit tugging at your sarong. You look quite fetching, wife . . ." Price said, one black eyebrow arching sardonically.

Lee watched him warily, then settled herself on the blanket he had spread near the fire, welcoming its warmth. As she lifted the glass to take a sip, Price dropped down next to her. Before she could swallow the wine and protest he had hitched himself close to her so his hip was touching hers. She cleared her throat. "I think I'd like to move away from the fire. Could you move, please?"

"Of course. Here, let me help you," Price said smoothly, hooking one arm around her waist and edging her back even closer to him.

"I think you know that isn't what I meant . . ." Lee said in frigid tones.

"It's good champagne, Lee," Price said, ignoring her other remark. "I'm amazed at the quality of New York State wines. I knew California had some fine ones but I never considered New York. This is fine. As fine as I've had anywhere."

Lee forgot her uneasiness at Price's closeness in her eagerness to tell him of the expanding wine business in her beloved Finger Lakes. She had no idea of the passage of time as she warmed to her subject, delighted in Price's knowledgeable questions. She hardly noticed when he eased her back against the log he had placed behind them. He was lying on his side propped on one elbow, watching her. She paused for breath, sipping at her almost empty glass.

"Let me fill that for you, Lee. Easy, your glass isn't level. You're spilling the wine." Price laughed as she struggled to sit straighter, tipping more wine onto the fire. "You're tipsy on two glasses of wine."

"Not either." Lee hiccupped a laugh, trying to take the bottle from him and spilling more, this time on Price. She put her free hand over her mouth, trying to control her giggles.

"Laughing at me, are you, wife?" Price growled, leaning over her. He took the glass from her hand and set it behind him. In the flickering firelight his tanned face was a sculpted Lucifer.

Too late Lee saw his intent and she put up her hands to ward him off. Her "No" was whispered against his mouth. Almost at once his mouth lifted, making her feel bereft, as they slid over her eyes and down her cheek. She held her breath, wanting him to kiss her, wanting to push him away. She felt his lips feather her ear, then press her neck, curving down to her throat. She could feel her blood thundering through her body. His lips stayed at her breast for long, agonizing moments, as she felt her resistance drifting away, his one hand loosening the edge of the towel wrapped around her. With one swift moment he pulled the other beach robe over the two of them and pulled the toweling away from her body. "Price," she gasped, trying to keep a shred of sanity.

"You're mine, Lee," he growled in her ear, amusement threading the unsteadiness in his voice. Then his mouth was on hers and she couldn't speak. He didn't hurry. His mouth seemed to drag from one pulsating part of her body to the next. Lee felt helpless under the onslaught. Then she seemed to hear, louder than the drumming of her pulses, the amused confidence in his voice when he told her she was his. Not that he loved her . . . but that she belonged to him and he intended to brand her again as his own.

He lifted his head, muttering, his breathing harsh. "Lee, my God, Lee . . . it's been so long . . ."

With a strength she didn't know she had, she shoved him away from her, making sure she pushed away from the fireside. She scrambled to her knees while Price watched her, for a moment dazed with his own feelings. "No, no, no. You won't do that to me again, Price. I'm not a thing owned by the organization or by you. Something you can use . . . then throw away," Lee sputtered, her teeth chattering with more than cold as she looked down on Price, who lay there, not bothering to hide his arousal.

"Are you a tease now, wife?" Price grated, staring up at her, violent tremors in his face. "Is that all it's been for you? Do you get your kicks by arousing men, then leaving?"

"Damn you, damn you. You know I'm not like that. I hate you, Price. You're an unmitigated bastard!" Lee rasped harshly.

He rose to his feet as though in slow motion. Then they stood facing each other, stiff and angry, like two antagonists in an arena. Fury pulsed between them. "I'm not giving you a divorce, Lee. You can tell that hayseed barrister that for me. Tell him, Lee, tell him how I can and will break him if he tries to go up against me."

"You filthy swine . . ." Lee choked, before snatching at her towel and running toward the driveway. She had only taken a few steps when an iron-hard hand closed on her elbow, making her stumble.

"Get in the jeep." Price bit the words at her.

Lee was sure he could hear the slow, loud drumroll of her heart as they ascended the steep curving drive in pulsing silence. When they arrived in front of the garage Price applied the brakes with such violence, she was almost catapulted from the seat. Without looking at him again, she rushed into the house and to her room. Stripping the wrapped towel from her body and throwing it to the floor she climbed between the sheets, her body shaking as though from ague.

She never remembered closing her eyes to sleep. She just rolled herself into a ball of misery, knowing her pain was even more intensified than when she had left Price the first time. Oh, God, how was she to escape him now? He would never let her go.

* * *

The sun bouncing off the white ceiling awakened Lee. At once she was aware of the lost feeling deep inside her and the reason for it. A wave of despair threatened to overwhelm her. She rubbed her forehead with one shaking hand as she forced herself to a sitting position. The phone rang before she could stand. "Hello? Yes, Grant, I'm awake . . . What? So soon? Yes, yes, I know it's best . . . but . . . no, no of course I don't want to change our plans. Yes, I'll drive into Rochester and have lunch with you." Lee placed the receiver back in the cradle, remembering Price's threats of last night. She would have to tell Grant what he said. Perhaps he wouldn't want to handle the case when she told him. Lee stepped under the shower, biting down hard on her lip as the icy water pelted her. No matter what, she was determined now to divorce Price. She knew she couldn't afford to let him see how affected she was by him. How he would laugh if he knew! He would try to take Rica away if he ever discovered how weak she was. She would stop him somehow, Lee vowed, turning the water on full with a vicious turn.

All during the trip into the city, she practiced what she would say to Grant. Lee tried to think of ways that she could reassure him about Price, persuade him not be intimidated by him. *That's a laugh,* she grated to herself, correcting the drift of the car as a driver coming the other way leaned angrily on his horn. *Who am I to tell Grant not to worry about Price, when the man has me scared witless? Why does Price have that effect on me?* she quizzed herself, hitting the steering wheel with her open palm. *Gladdy's right. I am not like that with anyone else. I'm just being childish,* she adjured herself. *It's just a holdover from our marriage. I'm getting the divorce,* she thought determinedly, *and nothing will stop me. I'll drop a rock on his head if he interferes with me.* She sighed, feeling slightly comforted.

Grant surprised her when he said that Price didn't scare him; that he would move for the divorce with greater speed. For some reason Lee wasn't reassured. In fact when Grant said he would fight Price, a frisson of fear rippled her spine. She wanted to cry out to Grant that Price would tear him to pieces, that he would chew him up and spit him out in four directions. She said nothing. The luncheon went badly even with all Grant's assurances. The food tasted like sawdust. Lee stared at her favorite shrimp salad, made with giant shrimps dredged in lemon juice and tossed with the lightest of dressings, and wondered why it tasted vile.

Grant didn't seem to notice her silence through the meal nor her palpable relief when they parted. He was too full of the grand plans he was making.

Lee watched his retreating figure wend its way down West Main Street to his office on Lawyer's Row and wondered why she felt so helpless.

When she returned to the house on the hill she felt a momentary satisfaction as she looked at its graceful blending with the surrounding Bristol Hills; the blue green of the spruce seeming to emphasize the rightness of natural cedar, the clean lines of the modern house an extension of nature itself.

Lee sighed, put the Celica in gear, and climbed the winding drive to the garage. She could see Rica jumping up and down waving her arms, with Price close behind her.

"Mommy, Mommy, Daddy is going to take Johnny and me to Roseland. You can come too," the child shouted, almost breathless with excitement.

"Darling, that's lovely . . . but I can't go. Gladdy is over in Canandaigua now with a friend and I told her I would pick her up this afternoon . . ." Lee began.

"No, Mommy, you can come, Daddy took care of it," Rica crowed, turning to run with Duke across the yard to where Johnny was coming up the hill.

Lee turned to Price, her lips pressed tight together to

keep from shouting at him. "And just what gives you the right to . . ."

"Cool down, Lee," Price interrupted, his smile twisted, his eyes hard. "Gladdy called here to see what time you were coming and told me about the famous Roseland. I suggested that we come early and all go to Roseland but it seems she has a meeting tonight. So *she* suggested that we drive two cars, then she can drive herself back. Unless of course you are so averse to me, you would deny your daughter an outing she is looking forward to having . . ." Price shrugged, looking her up and down in an insolent way.

"You know damn well I can't very well tell Rica, or Johnny either, that they can't go after you've told them that they can. What a typically high-handed Price Chatham trick," Lee hissed at him, clenching her hands to keep them from trembling.

"How was your luncheon with lover boy? Did you tell him to stuff the idea of divorce in his briefcase . . . or else I'd do it for him?" Price queried, biting the words off like they were metal.

"I said nothing of the kind. Well, that is, I told him that *you* didn't want to proceed with the divorce . . . but when he found that I did he said nothing would deter him. You can't scare everyone, Price."

"Can't I? We'll see." He turned away from her, his face hard. The rigid way he was holding himself was more threatening to her than mere words.

Lee had dreaded the forty-five-minute drive to the small resort city of Canandaigua but the constant chattering of Johnny and Rica glossed over the tension she was feeling. She could feel Price's eyes burning into her as he followed in the other car. Rica and Johnny played a game whereby they shouted and waved to Price driving behind them. Lee sighed with relief when they reached their destination.

Roseland was crowded on this warm summer's day.

The laughing screams from the roller coaster and the ferris wheel were a background for the other carny sounds. The first stop was the merry-go-round, where they met Gladdy. Johnny and Rica rode the giraffe and the tiger for three rides.

"I'm glad Price is riding with them, Lee. I'm like you. I don't like going round and round." Gladdy laughed, trying to eat the cotton candy Price had purchased for her. "I love this stuff, but it always gets in my eyebrows. Don't ask me to explain that. I can't."

Lee grimaced at the cloudlike swirl in pink that Gladdy held. "I can't abide cotton candy. I'm a hot-dog-and-mustard freak myself." Lee looked around at the bustling, smiling people. "I'd forgotten how much fun Roseland is. I haven't been here since I was a small girl. Mom and Dad brought me." Lee smiled at Johnny, who was trying to reach for the brass ring like the adults.

"Look, Lee, Price caught the brass ring," Gladdy said dryly, watching as he tossed it down into Lee's lap as she sat on the bench with her. "I like him, Lee. Oh, don't look ready to fight. I haven't turned on you. It just means I was prepared to hate him, but I found myself liking him instead. He's good to Rica and she loves him. I don't know what you two will do with your lives but I do know, for a fact, that Price is bound close to Rica and so are you. Be careful, Lee. I love you and want you to be happy."

Lee stared into Gladdy's concerned eyes and nodded slowly.

When they pried Johnny and Rica off the merry-go-round, Rica was insistant that she wanted to go on the roller coaster. Price was adamant in refusing to let her. For short moments Rica sulked, then rallied when her father told her that he would take Lee on the roller coaster and she and Johnny could sit with Gladdy and watch.

"Oh . . . no . . . I don't think so, Price," Lee said, glaring at him, already feeling butterflies in her stomach as she gazed upward at the speeding cars rattling around a curve at what, she privately thought, was a death-wish speed. "I don't really care to . . ."

"Oh, Mommy, go, you'll like it, won't she, Johnny?"

Johnny stared at his playmate for long seconds, then looked at Lee and nodded solemnly. Lee didn't feel reassured as she looked at a mirthful Gladdy standing there with one hand covering her mouth.

With a stiff nod, Lee conceded. When she tried to wrench her elbow out of Price's grip, hissing that she could manage to get up the ramp leading to the roller coaster without his help, he leaned over close to her and told her not to be a baby.

Seething, Lee climbed into the car, affixing the seat belt and the steel bar to lock her in before she noticed they had sat themselves in the front seat. Gasping, Lee tried to unfasten herself, but it was too late as Price dropped down beside her and locked himself in with her.

"Congratulations, darling, I didn't think you would have the chutzpah to choose the front seat." Price laughed at her open-mouthed horror as they started to move slowly, the car swaying gently from side to side. She was grateful when he settled his right arm tight around her as they began the first almost perpendicular climb.

"Price Chatham, for the first time in my life I hope I will be sick to my stomach," Lee hissed at him, through clenched teeth, wondering what the people behind them had to shout and laugh about as they teetered at the peak of the mountain-shaped track. Then she thought nothing as they hurtled in such a downward thrust she was sure she would be uprooted from her seat. She pushed her face into Price's chest as he wrapped both arms tight around her. She never opened her eyes once in the interminable bone-jarring ride, but it surprised her how safe she felt, caught close to Price. She lifted her face into his neck, praying silently he would hold her tighter. Unaccountably his arms did tighten. Lee pressed her mouth against the pulse in his throat, taking comfort from the rhythm.

"Darling, you can open your eyes now. Everyone has left and I think the man is waiting for us," Price whispered, amusement threading his voice.

Feeling disoriented, Lee allowed Price to lift her from the car, not looking at the custodian of the roller coaster in the face but noticing his grease-stained jeans and the black under his finger nails.

Lee felt like making a rude face at Gladdy when she congratulated her on how well she had ridden the roller coaster. Price's chuckle didn't improve matters. She followed blindly along after the children as they skipped just ahead of her. She was still feeling rocky when she bumped into Johnny as he stood watching a bearlike man in a sweaty tank shirt try to hit the target hard enough with a sledgehammer to ring the bell at the top of a high pole. After three attempts while they were watching he was only able to hit the mark three quarters of the way up, making the system buzz but not ring.

"My daddy can do better than that, can't he, Johnny?" Rica carolled into the sudden silence as the man braced himself, huffing and puffing over the long-handled hammer. The man turned slowly, glaring balefully at Rica just as Johnny nodded his head in slow-measured assent.

"Izzat so?" the winded man growled. "Well, let's just see him do better 'n'at," the bear man said, his crooked front teeth making him snarl, as he thrust the hammer at Price while pointing to the three-quarter mark on the pole.

Lee covered her hand to keep back a giggle as Gladdy made a disparaging remark about men with tufts of hair on their shoulders and in their noses and ears. "Yes, do go ahead and show them, Price, dear. The children are so proud of you," Lee said in saccharine tones.

Price's mocking gaze told her that he knew she was getting back at him for the roller coaster ride.

Without speaking, Price took the sledge and hefted it a few times, then brought it in a slow slow arc to the target without actually touching it. All at once he stepped back, brought the sledge up into the arc rapidly, swinging it in faster and faster circles, until he brought it to the target with a crashing twang that sent the ball up the pole, past the three-quarter mark to ring the bell with a resounding gong.

"Macho man," Lee muttered to herself under the noise of the cheering. She wanted to tell Gladdy not to clap her hand so gleefully and stop the children from jumping up and down.

Without a word the bear man left and Price collected his box of cigars, with the air of a man who always gets what he wants and is no longer surprised by the fact.

Lee was relieved when the children ran on ahead and she had the excuse to run after them and not speak to Price. Hearing outlandish squeaking up ahead, she forgot Price and sprinted to catch up with the children, who were pushing their way through a crowd of people. Open-mouthed, Lee looked at the huge corrallike structure that had been turned into a mud wallow. In the wallow a fair-sized pig was running and trying to escape from a mud-coated man who was trying to bring him down by tackling him. The pig seemed to be winning but tiring.

Before she could stop to think, Lee stepped up on the fence in front of the children. "Stop that at once. That poor animal is exhausted. Stop that. I mean it. If you tackle that animal again, I'll get the ASPCA down here. . . ." Lee pointed a finger at the man poised to make grab at the pig again. The animal stood head down, facing his adversary, sides heaving.

"Mind your own business, lady. This here ain't no part of the park. This here is private property and I say what goes on on my property."

"And I say you're breaking the law by being cruel to this animal, and I won't allow it." Lee gulped, seeing the bearlike man who had challenged Price come and stand next to the squat man talking to her.

The bearlike man told the mud-spattered man to go ahead with the duel with the pig.

All Lee's emotional upheavals seemed to surface at once, boiling to the top and over in one frustrated moment. Infuriated, she turned to Rica and told her to tell Gladdy to call the sheriff, then she vaulted over the fence into the wallow, sinking to her ankles in mud. Before the surprised men could act she was in front of the pig, who, for reasons known only to itself, did not move when Lee approached. "I am not moving from in front of this animal and if you, sir, dare to attack it in front of all these people, you will be taken to the court and found guilty of assault. You will go to prison," Lee pronounced, pointing an accusing finger at the mud-spattered man. Her hand was shaking as common sense asserted itself and she realized what an untenable position she had placed herself in.

"Go wan, Robbie, go for the pig. Don' pay no attention to that dumb broad. If she gets hurt, it's her own fault," the bear man growled.

"If you move against my wife, I will kill you, Robbie. Remember that." Price's voice was low but it carried to Robbie and all the spectators very clearly in the sudden silence. Price sat, straddled on the top of the fence, his face granite hard, the rest of him looking relaxed.

Lee didn't see Gladdy or the children and assumed that the older woman had taken the children away.

"You gonna take all us on, mister?" the mud-spattered man blustered.

"If that's the way it has to be," Price said, his voice still low, lifting his leg over so that he was sitting at the top, gripping the fence.

Lee thought he looked like a big cat poised to spring.

The bear man sidled up to the mud-spattered man, standing close to him, in a crouch.

Price seemed to fly from the top of the fence, feet first, his arms thrusting him out like a projectile. He caught both men in the chest with his feet, knocking the wind from them so that they stumbled and fell backward. Open-mouthed, Lee turned at a movement behind her, one hand swiping at the mud on her face. "Johnny, how did you get in here? Where are you going with the pig?"

Before the phlegmatic Johnny could answer her, Lee heard an angry shriek behind her. An irate, wide-hipped woman tried to shoulder past Lee, yelling to Johnny that that was her husband's pig. Appalled, Lee saw Rica behind Johnny, trying to coax the pig to go with her. Lee could hear Gladdy telling the children to come out of there at once.

"Don't you shout at those children." Lee grabbed at the woman's arm. The woman turned and stiff-armed Lee into the mud. As Lee felt herself falling she grasped the woman's arm and pulled her with her. From her vantage point in the mud, Lee watched Gladdy get the children out of the corral, the docile, quiet pig stepping daintily with them.

When the sheriff arrived and finally worked his way through the ring of spectators, Price was somehow able to make him listen. The upshot of it was that the squat man was to be cited for cruelty to animals. Price promised that the pig would be turned over to the ASPCA, despite the wails from Rica that she wanted to keep Mud as a pet.

"Mud?" Price quizzed Gladdy, his voice tired, as they reached the cars.

"She and Johnny have christened the pig Mud." Gladdy laughed, unfolding car blankets to spread over the car seats. "Not that the name wouldn't suit this whole family. Price! You're not going to drive in bare feet! Listen, you two, why don't you come to Myra's with me and the children. You could wash off there. I'm also going to call Johnny's mother and explain why I'm keeping the children overnight. She can cancel my meeting for me. Think about it, Price. There's room at Myra's."

"No, Gladdy, I'd better get this pig to Tom. He'll know how to pen it up until I can get it to the animal shelter,"

Price said, putting up the wire separator in the back of the station wagon.

Everyone held their breath until Price was able to lift the pig into the back of the vehicle.

"It's probably just as well that the children are staying at Myra's overnight. They were both exhausted," Lee said stiltedly, eliciting a noncommittal monosyllable from Price. They were well onto the highway before she spoke again, clearing her throat. "I didn't expect to see pig wrestling in this state. I didn't know they had it here."

"Um. Well, if you're trying to get rid of me, I think a divorce would be more effective . . ."

"You said you wouldn't divorce me," Lee answered tartly. "Besides, I didn't ask for your support today. I didn't think nice little English boys knew how to fight with their feet that way."

"Nice little English boys go to tough grammar schools that teach them how to survive," Price said dryly. "Whatever happened to the cool cucumber I married who would never involve herself in anything so earthy, no pun intended, as a pig wrestle?"

"I was never a snob, Price," Lee bristled. "With you I was awkward. You made me feel as though I had two left feet, that I was gauche and unsophisticated."

"That's not true, Lee." Price frowned, maneuvering around a truck piled high with egg cartons.

"Oh, yes, it's true. I was not the one you included when you engaged in that clever banter that was so much a part of your life when we lived in London. I was the afterthought." Lee gulped, fighting to keep the hurt from surfacing and letting Price know how raw such memories could still make her feel.

"Damn you, you're wrong, Lee. I gave up most of those so-called sophisticated friends after we married. I didn't think you'd like them. I always tried to include you in the rest of my life," Price grated. "I let my associates do most of the . . . *ah-choo* . . . the traveling after we were married . . . *ah-choo.*" Price sniffed, lifting one hand to wipe his eyes.

"You're catching a cold. We should have stayed at Myra's. She has more room than she can handle in her old house. We should have stayed. You know how susceptible you are," Lee said.

"Damn you, Lee, I'm susceptible to nothing. I'm strong as a horse . . . never been sick a day in my life . . ." Price barked, furious with her, dull red coloring his cheekbones.

"Until you had pneumonia," Lee said stiffly, feeling breathless as she watched his knuckles whiten on the wheel. "The minute we get home you must . . ."

"Don't coddle me," Price shouted, surprising Lee, who had never heard her cool, worldly, cynical husband shout.

Then it came to her like a flame in the darkness. Price had been embarrassed by his illness. It had thrown him for a loss not to be on top of everything for once, not to be in complete command of the situation. To Lee it made him somehow more human and vulnerable, like the rest of the human race. "You are going in the hot tub when we get home . . . or I'll call Doctor Spellman . . ."

"Don't threaten me, Lee," Price grated, then started to cough. "I'll be fine as soon as I get out of these wet clothes and get that darn pig taken care of . . ."

"Then the hot tub," Lee stated, feeling reckless, when a grim-faced Price floored the accelerator, making the wagon jump forward like a jack rabbit.

"Damn you, Lee, if I wasn't driving this car . . ."

"You're not driving it . . . you're firing it like a projectile. We hydroplane on these hills and Rica will be an orphan," Lee said, pleased that her voice sounded cool.

The speed lessened at once but Price's face looked murderous. "I never tried to exclude you from my life," Price said harshly. "You were the one that decided to end it. Not me. You were the one that walked, leaving me to wonder where you were, if you were all right, if you were safe. What a hell you put me through by indulging your imagination! You skinned me alive, Lee, time after time after time. What the hell have you to complain of after what you did to me!" Price coughed, then cleared his throat. "Now it's your turn to pay the piper, darling. You're going to stay with me, live with me. Perhaps by the time Rica is a grown woman I may decide to let you go . . . but you are not leaving me again, Lee, nor am I leaving here." He paused for a moment. "Unless you're with me, that is. I have a conference in New York later this month about the merger. You'll be with me, Lee."

Lee, about to explode over the ruthless way he was disposing with her future, held her tongue when he began to cough again.

Still seething when they arrived back at the hilltop, Lee slammed out of the car, her lips pressed into a tight line. *I'm going to weight him down with a huge rock and drop him in the lake one day,* she planned, gleefully picturing a bubbling, sinking Price.

Lee switched on the hot tub in an alcove of the bedroom wing, where floor to ceiling bow windows opened on to a panoramic vista of the surrounding Bristol Hills and the lake below. Mumbling angrily to herself she stripped off her mud-caked clothing, hearing the rise and fall of Tom and Price's voices as they decided where to place Mud. She was still muttering to herself as she stepped under the shower adjacent to the laundry room. Lee had felt she was too dirty to attempt to use the shower in her own bathroom. She scrubbed herself hard with a loofah sponge, feeling some of her angry tension drain away with the dirt.

As she shampooed her hair, she felt a cold draft on her body. Stiffening, she realized someone had opened the shower door, but she'd gotten shampoo in her eyes and couldn't see who it was.

"Darling, I must tell you that I like that peachy skin

without clothes . . ." Price's laughing voice was interrupted by a cough.

Even under the shower Lee could feel her body heating up at the thought of Price observing her nudity. "Price . . . please," she pleaded, trying to open her eyes. "Get into the hot tub. It's ready for you. I'll be along in a moment . . ."

"First, like you, I have to wash off some of this dirt. That's it, wife, move over. Ummm, now doesn't that feel good. Here, let me scrub your back. You have perfect skin, Lee . . . soft . . . glowing . . ."

Lee felt herself trembling as Price continued to massage her with the loofah. Her limbs felt like melting wax. With great effort she levered herself away from Price and stepped from the shower.

She toweled herself with shaking fingers, wrapping another towel around her hair. It was an effort not to watch Price as he finished shampooing his hair.

She escaped to her room and sat on the bed, pushing her face into her hands. Why had she let him get to her like this? Why had she allowed him to wield that old power over her? *Old power, hell,* she told herself. His hold over her was more potent now than it had ever been. She shivered in self-disgust as she thought of the covetous way she'd looked at his naked body. *Is he just going to whistle and you'll come to heel?* she scourged herself.

"Do you feel ill, Lee?" It was Price. He'd opened the door of her room.

She jumped to her feet, clutching at her slipping towel. "No . . . just a little reaction maybe, from all the excitement. Perhaps it's just as well that the children stayed at Myra's . . . Oh, I forgot to call the Greenways . . ."

"I took care of it," Price said, his voice calm compared to the green wildness of his eyes. "Is there anything special I should know about the hot tub? Show me."

Lee wanted to tell him to figure it out himself but the barely controlled violence in his face kept her silent. She felt his anger even across the room. *What's eating him?* she wondered irritably. *I'm the one being torn to pieces.*

She instructed Price to step down into the tub after they had walked in silence from the bedroom to the alcove. She was still wrapped in her towel, intending to dress as soon as Price was in the hot tub. As she showed him the control panel on the rim of the tub, he clamped his hand on her arm. Before she could do more than gasp he had lifted her down into the hot swirling water. "Price . . . what are you doing . . . my towel," Lee squeaked, gulping as she was submerged to her neck, Price's arms enclosing her.

"In Japan, families often bathe together," he whispered against her earlobe.

"I'm sure when you were in Japan, you didn't even bother with family. Just picked some young thing and . . ." Lee sputtered, jealousy knifing through her at the thought.

"I imagine you could do that anywhere, not just Japan," Price drawled.

"What?" Lee turned toward him, her temper heating as fast as the water.

"That's better," Price growled. "Don't pull back, Lee. Kiss me."

"No," Lee quavered, her eyes riveted on the sensuous twist of his mouth.

"Kiss me, Lee."

Lee could only obey, the censorious inner voice smothered by the bone-shaking desire to be close to him. At the first tentative touch, her mouth came alive, its mobility fitting to his as though their lips had been made to fit. Her hand lifted through the water to his chest, her fingers pulling at the crisp wet curls. When she heard him gasp, she felt sensuous power surge through her. His hands came up to caress her breasts and even in the warm water she felt her nipples harden in his hands.

All at once he swept to his feet, holding Lee in one arm. "It's been too long, Lee. I have to make love to you, darling. Now." He reached for a fluffy beige bath sheet, cocooning her, then stepped dripping and naked onto the carpeting surrounding the tub. His face like carved granite, he walked, unsmiling, to the bedroom, holding her high against his chest.

He stood her on her feet, patting her dry with the bath sheet. "Dry me, darling," he requested tenderly when he'd finished.

"Price . . ." Lee began, feeling her heart thud painfully as she looked at him.

"No objections, Lee, I'm in no mood to listen."

She lifted the towel around him and began drying his body. Before she got to his waist, Price's face was suffused with dark color and he was breathing as though he'd been running. Lee's mind shut off. She was immersed in pleasure. It was as though she had been given something she had been waiting for forever . . . Price. Her lips parted on an aching sob as Price kissed her. His kiss deepened. As they fell on the bed together, the towel dropped to the floor.

"God, Lee, I've wanted you," Price groaned as he let his mouth rove over her aroused body.

With restless hands she gripped him tightly, trying to bring him to her as the blood raced through her veins. She felt as though her body was being swept away by an enormous tide.

"Is this what you want, darling?" Price crooned to her as he lifted himself over her. "Tell me."

"Yes, yes, yes," Lee choked, pressing her lips to his throat, her restless hands stroking him.

"Slowly, my angel, slowly," Price breathed into her hair. "I've waited too long for you. I want to savor this moment." His mouth nuzzled its way to her navel, then he lifted his head to look at her, his eyes a liquid fire. "Your body is perfect. Your waist is like a little girl's, but here . . ." His one hand teased her breast, her nipple, then let the fullness fill his hand. ". . . You're all woman. Do you know how many times I would lie in my bed and think of you like this?" His voice had a hoarseness. "Your hips are so small. How did you ever have a baby?" he mused, his eyes following his hands as they curved over her hips, a double exploration of the caves and valleys of her body.

Lee's body clenched and arched as his heated hands directed her toward him. Her own hands pulled and plucked at the soft mat on his chest. She could see the faint gray stubble on his chin that no amount of shaving ever erased. She marked every pore with finger and eye. She could remember how much she had loved him and how shy she had often been with him. She felt no shyness now. She felt an overwhelming need to pull him with her into the eye of hurricane.

Her sudden aggression made his heart thunder over hers as she felt his surprise and instant response to it.

"Darling, don't stop. God, where did you learn that?" he groaned into her neck, his body lifting over hers.

Lee could hear the husky voice calling out Price's name and for long moments she didn't recognize it as her own as his taut body positioned into hers. The sudden shock of ecstasy stunned her, and she raked her nails into his shoulders. They spiraled together, clinging and entangled, her hideaway world splintering.

Price woke her once more in the night, his mouth at her breast. Her nipples hardened at once as she lifted her arms to enclose him. She had not yet opened her eyes.

"I will never have enough of you, wife," Price muttered, his hands and mouth grooving to her body.

Lee sighed, her body arching and eager. Again she felt the mounting excitement, his thrusting body giving her a mindless joy.

Afterward, he wrapped her in his arms, her sleep a deep and dreamless one.

CHAPTER FOUR

Half-asleep, Lee reached for the ringing phone. It took a few moments before she realized that the warmth she felt at her back was Price. She kept her voice to a whisper when she spoke. "Yes? Oh, yes, Grant. Oh, I'm sorry. I was away most of yesterday. That's why you were unable to reach me. Listen, let me get back to you on the kitchen phone. No, no reason, I just haven't had my coffee."

She pressed the button for the kitchen pickup and eased herself from the bed, smiling as she watched Price burrow deeper into the bed, his breathing slow and steady, his lips slightly parted. She felt a fluttering in her chest as she looked at him . . . a shaky delight.

In the kitchen, she lifted the receiver and assembled the percolator at the same time. The phone amplifier permitted her to set the table and get things from the refrigerator while she was listening to Grant. "Yes, yes of course I'm listening . . ." she assured him as she reached to steady a tumbling glass.

"Well, it looks as though I have the ball rolling. I've had an agreement drawn up for a separation. We have asked him for nothing, Lee. Now, I have other good news . . ."

Lee stiffened as she heard a distinct click on the line. Had Price heard their conversation? "What? Oh, yes, What was it you said? Yes, I am a little foggy this morning."

"Tansy wants you to bring Gladdy and Tom and the

Greenways to her home for the cocktail party before the cotillion. I told her you wouldn't come without them, since they were helping you on the committee. Wasn't that nice of her?"

"Darling. But, Grant, since the cotillion is this coming Saturday and I think Price will be still here, I won't be able to leave him behind . . ."

"Oh, very well, bring him. I think it's ridiculous that he stays on where he knows he isn't wanted. I'll bring Grace Moreland along to balance the numbers. The man's a damned nuisance, Lee. I hope he knows how to behave. The Durhams will be coming as well and old man Durham hinted that he might want to talk to me about the Scanlon deal. If he wants me to handle it personally, it will be quite a coup, dear. I don't need to tell you what this could mean for us. The Durhams are important people. Lee? Lee?"

Lee mumbled something into the phone, then as soon as she was able, broke the connection. She couldn't take her eyes off Price, standing in the doorway, one hand moving through unruly hair, the other clenching and unclenching, as if to control his inner violence.

"You listened," Lee accused, her chin lifting in defiance.

"Yes, I listened. And a good thing too." Price bit out the words. "What was that last night, Lee? A softening up for the blow? Hell, you needn't have bothered, lady, I'm as tough as Welsh coal . . ."

"I am perfectly aware of how *hard* you are . . ." Lee sputtered.

"Then just remember it . . . and tell lover boy that I'm signing nothing and that you're signing nothing. I'll break him, Lee, I mean it. If you try to divorce me, I'll fight you every step of the way. I think the courts will be understanding about a man who wants to be with his child, especially after the child has been hidden from him. I hold some strong cards, Lee. I'll play them, never doubt it."

"You wouldn't . . . you couldn't take Rica away from me," Lee gasped, her pulse accelerating with fear.

"I have no intention of taking Rica from you unless you force my hand. I'm telling you here and now. After this . . . this cotillion or whatever it is . . ."

"It's the annual dance, held every year in the county. The Greenways and I were on the committee this year. Betty Greenway has been handling most of it since your arrival," Lee told him dazedly.

"All right. After the cotillion, you're coming with me to New York. We'll be there a couple of weeks. After that, Gladdy will bring Rica to New York to join us, then we'll go to England to see my father. Lieber will be told by me that our marriage is no longer his concern . . ."

"No, I have to tell him. He'll be so hurt . . ." Lee began.

"Tough."

"You heartless bastard." Lee pushed past him as she rushed from the kitchen.

She stood on the patio, looking out over the lake but seeing nothing, her stomach knotting painfully. Why had she let down her guard? Why had she let him get close to her again? *A psychiatrist would have a field day with you, Lee old girl,* she told herself bitterly.

To Lee's relief, Gladdy returned with the children late that morning and the flurry of their activities with the dog allowed Lee to keep her distance from Price. Not that ignoring his existence helped much. She had the very real feeling that he had somehow crawled under her skin and lodged there.

The following days she was unable to concentrate on her writing. Every time she sat at the typewriter, Price's face was there in front of her. Finally she called Betty Greenway and told her that she was coming with her to help with the decorations at the club.

"But, Lee, you don't need to come unless you wish. I

know how busy you've been with your husband being ill . . ."

"He's fine now. I really want to help, Betty. I'll pick you up this afternoon."

The afternoon was hectic and physically taxing. It was just what Lee needed. When she and Betty had strung the last of the Chinese lanterns around the pool, they sat down to some sandwiches that the club chef had thoughtfully provided.

"Oh, God, Lee, get your sandwich down fast. Here comes Little Miss Indigestion herself," Betty said dryly.

Without turning her head, Lee knew that Tansy Culver was heading her way. She sighed, too weary to care.

"Lee? I'm surprised you're here. Every day that I've been here, you've been missing . . . but . . . I understand you have domestic problems."

"Tansy, if you're looking for work, why not go out and help the men groom the golf course. You could do it with manicure sicissors," Betty said brightly.

Tansy looked at the two women balefully. "Do not try to be funny, Betty. You fail miserably." She smoothed down the front of her cotton skirt. "Since you are on the committee, you are both invited to my cocktail party."

"Whoopee," Lee said, twirling one finger over her head.

"Really, Lee, you are so childish. I don't know what my brother sees in you," Tansy pronounced waspishly. "Good day."

The two women watched, chin in hand, as an irritated Tansy swept from the room.

"For two pins I wouldn't go to her stupid party," Lee muttered, yawning.

"You have to go. I want to see her house. You can't let down your nosy friend," Betty said complacently, biting down on a dill pickle.

"Twenty lashes with a wet noodle for nosy friends who want to look in houses. Come on, let's go home. I want to nap before I have to face Tansy and that gaggle of geese she's invited."

Betty laughed and followed her out to the car, still munching on a pickle.

After dropping Betty at her house, Lee drove home and showered. Donning a silky wrap, she fell onto the bed and promptly fell asleep.

She barely heard the murmuring voice. It was Rica, of course. Not opening her eyes, she answered, "Yes . . . a'right, honey. You'll stay at Johnny's. Millie will be there. Yes, lie down with me. Good girl."

Sleep enveloped her once again, and she accepted it gladly. When she opened her eyes later, she felt rested, relaxed. There was a warmth at her bare back. She wondered hazily where her robe was, then belatedly realized that it had crept up almost to her shoulders. She turned to look into Price's sleeping face. With a startled expletive she tried to pull free of his encircling arm, but it only tightened around her. Price's eyelids lifted, his mouth a sardonic twist as he looked at her. Oh, how she hated that look!

With great effort he stifled a yawn. "Don't look so indignant, wife. You invited me into your bed," he mocked.

Lee tugged at her robe, trying to cover herself. "Don't be ridiculous. I did no such thing. Get off my robe," she snapped.

"Why? You don't need it. And you did invite me into your bed. When Rica and I came up from swimming, you were nodding off. I asked about the baby-sitter, then asked if I might lie down with you. You said yes."

Lee swallowed with difficulty, furious with him. "You know damn well I thought I was talking to Rica. Take that nasty smile off your face."

"I think you should stop arguing with me and get dressed. Look at the time."

His laughter followed her as she ran for the bathroom, forgetting in her hurry to clutch her robe to her.

Lee began to prepare herself for the cotillion by applying delicate shadings of makeup to her face and eyes. She held the dress she had chosen in front of her and looked into the mirror. She had definite misgivings. Scylla had talked her into buying the gown in London years ago when they had made one of their lightning forays into a designer house. Lee had never worn it, deeming it too daring. The style was timeless and starkly simple, but it was outrageous for the Bristol Country Club, she mused. The dress was sheerest silk, swathed tight to the knee, where it flared to the ankle, and sewn all over with the tiniest sequins that reflected a watery turquoise sheen from the black silk. It was an iridescent, Dali-esque effect, delicate but bewitching. There was no back, the material V-ing at her spine. The halter was a thin scarf of sequins about her neck. The dress V-eed again at the front almost to the navel.

Gladdy gave a soundless whistle when she came in to arrange Lee's hair. "You are going to knock them out of their socks, Lee. I like it." The two women laughed together as Lee eased herself into the chair in front of the mirror and Gladdy arranged her hair in a braided crown and soft, tendrillike curls falling loosely around her face. When Gladdy scurried off to get her earrings, which she had forgotten, Lee affixed her own opal drops, which swung against her cheeks as she moved. Besides her wedding ring, the only other jewelry she wore was an opal ring her father had given her. She twirled once in front of the mirror and took a deep breath. *Well, here goes!*

She picked up her black silk clutch bag from the dressing table just as the bedroom door opened and Price entered the room, a box in his hand. He pushed the door closed behind him, his eyes touching her everywhere at least twice. Lee didn't move.

"Gladdy tried to describe the dress when I asked her

about the color. She's right. It can't be described. You're exquisite, Lee. I'll be the envy of every man there. I hope they don't go wild. Here. Gladdy said there wouldn't be too many places to put a corsage so I brought you a wristlet. If you don't want them, just put them aside. You certainly don't need them," Price said, his voice sardonic.

Lee winced, but the warmth in his eyes gave her confidence as she reached for the flowers. They were tiny white roses—elegant, Lee thought. Then she noticed the plain black jeweler's box under the flowers as she lifted them. She looked inquiringly at Price but his face was a mask.

The box snapped open to reveal a narrow circle of gold nesting on white velvet. "Price, what a beautiful bracelet! But, you shouldn't . . ."

He fastened a hand to her waist and pulled her close, his lips pressing cool and light on hers. "Don't you know that you shouldn't question gifts from your husband? Any man gets pleasure in giving things to a beautiful woman. Leave it at that. Besides, you might think it's too much with both the flowers and bracelet . . ." He shrugged, watching her closely.

"I'm wearing both," Lee said firmly, and he laughed, his warm approval making her tingle as she fastened the bracelet.

"Shall we go, lovely lady? I understand we are to pick up the Greenways before we attend the cocktail party."

Lee nodded, feeling happy, rubbing one thumb against the smoothness of the bracelet.

Hank and Betty Greenway kept the talk going all the way to Tansy's house. Lee was grateful. She felt too confused by her own feelings to converse intelligently.

Tansy's house was situated amid a cluster of homes with well-manicured lawns called Crestwood Estates. It had a "nouveau riche" look to it, as though no expense had been spared to keep it ahead of its neighbors. Tansy had told Lee it had been patterned after a French château.

Price took Lee's hand as they stepped through the front

door. In the flurry of introductions, she was only able to nod to Grant but she knew that he had seen Price holding her hand. She excused herself to freshen up with Betty in the powder room. When they rejoined the party, Betty was stopped by a friend. Lee continued out to the patio. She took a drink from a passing tray and watched the patterns the sun was making on the bluish luminescence of the pool surface. She started when she felt a touch on her arm.

"Lee? How are you, dear?" Grant's smile changed as he looked her up and down. When he leaned down to kiss her, Lee turned her face without thinking, so that his kiss landed on her cheek. "Is something wrong, Lee? Are you angry because I was busy the other evening?"

Lee turned to face him fully, her skirt winging out around her. Her assurances that she wasn't angry died in her throat when she saw his lips purse in displeasure.

"Really, dear, I think Tansy is right about your clothes. That dress is not . . . well, it doesn't fit in here at the Bristols. It's too . . ."

"Oh, you don't say? Is it too sophisticated to compete with Tansy's prom frock?" Lee's voice shook with anger.

Before Grant could answer, she felt a familiar arm circle her waist, Price's mouth in her hair. For once she felt relieved at his presence and allowed her body to sag against him.

"Hello, Lieber. I think your sister wants you to speak with someone talking to her husband. Durham, I think the name is. Let me freshen your drink, darling. Tonic and lemon again?"

Lee nodded, relaxing now that Grant had left. She moved around the pool nodding to acquaintances, noting not a few raised eyebrows. The thought that perhaps she should go home and change was quickly squashed. She lifted her chin and smiled as a drink was pushed into her hand.

"Have I told you that you are the loveliest lady here?

I'm proud to be your escort," Price said quietly, as though he had known of her misgivings.

Lee looked up at him and felt a surge of confidence like a warm flood. She turned to the couple nearest them and introduced Price. In minutes he was telling one of the urbane, witty stories that were so much a fabric of his personality and his father's. Lee had forgotten how easily the inbred courtesy of the Chathams seeped to the surface until she caught the entranced gazes thrown Price's way by the women and the interested looks of the men. Nestled in his arm, his one hand brushing her bare back, she felt contented and safe.

Betty Greenway's whispered reminder that they should be going made her pull reluctantly away from him.

"What is it, love?" he said. "Time to leave? No problem. We'll make our good-byes to our hosts."

Once in the car, Lee gave Price directions on how to reach the club, talking over the excited chatter of Betty in the backseat, telling her husband she preferred her own house to Tansy's.

When Price reached over a hand and covered hers as it sat on the seat, Lee didn't move or try to disengage herself. She knew she would be angry with herself later but at the moment it felt wonderful to be close to Price and not to be arguing with him.

In too short a time they were at the club, seeing to the last-minute list proffered by the major domo. When the crowd came, it seemed to come as one piece of laughing humanity. The dinner went well. Lee judged this by the many nodding faces and approving smiles. She signaled to Betty with a wink and received a smile back. People began drifting to the dance floor before total darkness fell on the long summer's evening. The crowd seemed to enjoy dancing on the patio that balconied the pool.

Lee took a deep breath of satisfaction and turned to see Grant grimly making his way through the throng to her. She waited, her lower lip caught between her teeth.

"You'll have the first dance with your husband, Lee. To hell with Lieber," Price drawled in her ear, just before he twirled her out onto the patio.

Lee closed her eyes on Grant's tight-lipped irritation and leaned against Price. The music and the wine she had drunk with dinner gave her a floating feeling. Price fitted her closer to his body, his one hand rubbing slowly up and down her spine. She felt a light film of moisture bead her upper lip. Her hand had a life of its own as it stroked his neck.

"Do you remember the disco in London, Lee? Our first night together? The songs they played?" Price whispered huskily against her ear.

"Yes. Yes, I remember. I . . . I love dancing," Lee choked.

"You're a very good dancer, wife. Light. You move beautifully." Price leaned back for a moment to smile into her eyes. The music changed but Price didn't release her. Their bodies swayed to a beguine rhythm as though they couldn't dance apart.

Lee blinked when she saw a hand pass her face and tap Price on the shoulder.

"If you don't mind, Chatham . . . ?"

"Oh, but I do, Lieber." Price's voice was soft but there was a hot look to his eyes that worried Lee.

"It's all right, Price. I'll dance with Grant," she mumbled, not looking at her husband, but turning at once to Grant and urging him away.

Lee had to stifle a sigh as she tried to fit her steps to Grant's formula stiffness. After Price's sophisticated expertise, Grant was rough going. When he tried to speak to her they were too close to the band and Lee couldn't hear him. She watched his lips move for a moment, then shrugged helplessly. Frustrated, he led her back to a table where his sister and her husband sat surrounded by friends.

Lee pulled back. "No, I don't want to sit over there, Grant."

"Lee, don't be difficult. We have to talk. Come along. You can make conversation with Tansy and her friends for a short time, then you and I will . . ."

"No, Grant, I'm sorry," Lee interrupted, her voice firm. "I'm not going to sit at Tansy's table. Excuse me, I want to go to the powder room." Lee left him, feeling taut and white-faced. *I am fed up to the teeth with men,* she fumed to herself. *I feel like taking Rica and escaping to a desert island.* She began to reapply her lip gloss and then sat back for a minute, looking at her image in the mirror. *Tell me, funny lady in the mirror*—Lee grimaced at her reflection—*how do I get my life back on keel? How do I fight the sick feeling that comes over me at the thought of Price going out of my life forever? How do I live with him in my life, knowing that he'll never really belong to me?* The lady in the mirror was silent. Lee made a face at her and rose to leave the powder room.

"Lee? I've been waiting for you," Grant said stiffly. "I think that you could leave now. I've talked to Betty Greenway and she said there was nothing that she couldn't handle."

Lee turned to him, wanting to tell him she thought he was pretty high-handed, but when she saw the set expression on his face, she thought better of it. Besides, he was right. It was time they talked. She took a deep breath and nodded. "All right. Just let me say my good-byes to Gladdy and Tom."

"I've said them for you," Grant said promptly. "And the Greenways will be going home with Chatham."

Lee was relieved she wouldn't have to say anything to Price. She also believed it was time she talked to Grant. More and more she was becoming convinced that marriage to him was out of the question. She didn't delve too deeply into her feelings for Price, because she knew she was still very much confused on that issue. But to complicate her life even more by marriage to another man was out of the question.

The ride back to Highland Farms was punctuated by monosyllabic remarks that only added to Lee's discomfort. Once at the house she went directly to the kitchen, taking a jug of lemonade from the refrigerator. "Would you like yours with vodka or gin, Grant?"

"Vodka. I'll get it."

Drinks in hand, they wandered out to the patio. Lee took a deep swallow of the lemonade, savoring the citric bite in her throat.

"We're alone, I hope," Grant said. "Gladdy was still at the dance when we left and Chatham was dancing with Lally Gilbert. Perhaps she'll divert him long enough for us to have a talk," he added with wry satisfaction.

Lee winced at the jealous feeling that consumed her. *Damn the man that he could still cause her so much discomfort! Damn all men!* she thought, taking a swallow of lemonade and coughing as the tartness grabbed at her throat. "Grant. Uh . . . uh, excuse me. Swallowed the wrong way. Grant, I've been thinking a great deal about us . . . and . . . I don't think it would be right for us to marry. Wait, please. There are too many problems, too many questions unanswered, too many corners to turn. It just wouldn't work. I think we should just forget the whole thing and remain friends," Lee finished lamely.

Grant's face seemed to swell, mottling a deep red. He blinked once, his teeth coming together hard. "Everyone in this area knows that you and I are contemplating marriage, Lee. We had plans. You can't back out now. My name means something around here and I won't let you or anyone else make it a laughingstock." He was shouting at her now, striking his first into his palm.

"I have no intention of making you a laughingstock," Lee explained, keeping her voice low. "You break the news to everyone. Say that you broke it off with me. It doesn't matter to me."

"It matters to me. What changed your mind all of a sudden?" Grant snarled, his anger making his nostrils flare. "Was it Chatham? I knew he shouldn't have stayed here so long. How long did it take him to talk you into his bed . . ."

"Grant!" Lee exploded, anger coursing through her, more pronounced because Grant had come so close to what was bothering her. "You have no right to speak to me in such a fashion. I'm trying to be honest with you. I'm also trying to do what's right for Rica. I feel that the battleground of a divorce right now could be very damaging for her . . ." A slight breeze made Lee shiver. She returned to the lounge, switching on a table lamp.

"Is it Rica? Or is it that you don't think you can be parted from Chatham?" Grant snapped, following on her heels.

"I'm trying to explain but I can see that you have your own fixed ideas. Perhaps it's just as well that we found out now that we are so unsuitable for each other, isn't it?" Lee said, white-lipped.

"Don't you patronize me!" Grant shouted, his hands clenching and unclenching in mounting anger.

Startled, Lee looked at him open-mouthed, realizing that he was furious. Not thinking, she reached out a hand to touch his arm as though to placate him, but with a furious movement of his hand, he thrust her away. Off-balance, she staggered back, the high heel of her sandal giving way under her. Her arm flailed as she tried to save herself. Her cheek struck the edge of the table in front of the fireplace. She saw stars. Dimly she heard Grant call her name. Then he was lifting her unto the couch.

"Lee, are you all right? I'm so sorry. It was an accident."

Lee pressed a hand to her cheek, nodding. "Of course it was, Grant. I know that. I think I'd like to go to bed. Would you mind going now?"

Grant stepped back from the couch, looking down at

her, a frown on his face. "Damn him. It's all Chatham's fault. We were fine until he came here, Lee." He turned on his heel and stalked to the door.

Lee thought he had gone until he returned with an ice bag in his hand.

"Thank you, Grant. That's just what I needed."

"Do you need any help getting to your bed?" Grant asked.

"No, I don't need any help. I don't feel too badly. I just want to sleep."

She had the feeling he might have said more, but a throbbing head made her close her eyes and turn her face into the back of the sofa. She heard his footsteps retreat toward the door. She sighed when she heard the Mark V roar out the driveway. She pressed the ice against her face, pretty sure that she would have a black eye the next day. She rose to her feet some time later to replenish the ice that was melting in the bag. Standing at the kitchen sink, she let the cold water run over the wrist of one hand while she held the newly filled bag to her face.

"What the hell are you doing, Lee?" Price's harsh question made her whirl away from the sink with a gasp, still clutching the ice bag to her face. She watched his eyes narrow on her. "You had an accident. What happened to you? Tell me." He strode to her side and leaned down to scoop her up into his arms. "Relax. Hold onto your ice bag. That's a good girl. Put your arm around my neck. Here we go."

Her mumbled protests faded away at the comfort she felt in those strong, sure arms. When he placed her on the bed she lay back, feeling mute and helpless.

With a minimum of fuss, Price undressed her, ignoring her red-faced assurances that she could do it herself. She watched as though disembodied as he pawed through her dresser, pulled her frilliest nightgown from the drawer, and eased it over her head. It annoyed her a bit that he could be so calm about undressing her, that his face had a flat, unruffled look when he gazed at her naked body. With grating detachment he pulled the sheet up to her chin, then sat down on the edge of her bed. "Lee, don't go to sleep yet. I must know what happened to you." There was a strange throb in his voice, a flicker of something in the back of his eyes.

Lee eyes fluttered as she tried to concentrate. She swallowed, but her mouth was dry. She tried to moisten her lips with her tongue.

"Lee? Lee, tell me what happened." Price spaced his words.

She blinked, lifting restless fingers to her swollen face, still cold from the ice bag. "Grant . . ." she began, swallowing again.

Angry color ran under Price's skin, his eyes an emerald glitter. "Lieber? What about him?"

"He brought me home. We were talking. It was an accident," Lee pronounced in measured tones, her voice reedy.

"And?"

"It was an accident. He pushed my arm away. I tripped and fell against the coffee table. That's all. I'll be fine tomorrow." She licked her lips, watching Price.

His face was flint hard, his mouth a slash of rage. He looked as though he was in the grip of a searing emotion. "He struck you?" he whispered hoarsely.

"No, no, Price, he didn't strike me. He just pushed my arm away. I staggered and fell. That's the truth," Lee pleaded, trying to struggle upright as she looked at his contorted face.

With gentle hands he placed her back against the pillows, his firm lips pressing against her forehead. Unbidden tears pushed past her eyelids. When Price leaned back and saw the tears, a groan tore from him. As though he couldn't help himself, he gathered her into his arms and lowered himself to lie beside her. With a grateful sigh, Lee turned her face into his chest, her body relaxing against him. She felt herself drift into sleep. She wanted to tell Price not to let her go but she didn't have the strength.

Once in the night she woke, thinking she heard voices arguing. She realized she had been dreaming. She turned her head in a restless way and her mouth landed on a bare chest covered with curling hair. Her eyelids fluttered in confusion as she tried to orient herself. Price. She remembered him lying down beside her. Now he was asleep next to her, naked. She raised her hand to push him away. He muttered something in his sleep and tightened his arms around her. Satisfied she had done her best to repulse him, she nuzzled closer, falling into a deep sleep again.

When she woke once more, she heard the strong beat of his heart under her cheek. She was still enfolded tight to his body. Lifting her face from his shoulder, she looked up straight into his eyes, which were now almost a bayberry green in their opaqueness.

"Did you sleep well, Lee? Have you a headache?" he whispered.

She shook her head no, a tingling awareness of him rendering her speechless. She took a deep breath, surprised to find that she did feel good. She felt rested. Other than a soreness on her right hip and a throbbing stiffness in her face, she had a sense of well-being.

Price lifted his hand to her hair, brushing it gently back from her face. "I'm taking you to the hospital this morning," he declared. "I want a doctor to look at your head. You may need X rays."

When Lee tried to say something, Price placed two fingers on her lips and shook his head.

"There is no use arguing with me, Lee. You're seeing a doctor. I have some business in town myself."

When Lee looked at him inquiringly, he just shook his head and leaned over her, kissing her swollen face very gently. Lee's insides turned right over. She felt a dizzy wonder at the thought of being in bed with Price again after all the years apart, waking up in his arms. Liquid heat surged through her veins. She turned her face away, not wanting him to see how affected she was by his presence in her bed.

"Come on, lazybones. Up you get," Price said, lifting her to a sitting position.

Lee looked around at him, her face flushed, her eyes going over him restlessly.

Price paused in the act of swinging his legs to the floor, his eyes narrowing on her face, looking at each of her features as though they were telling him something.

She turned her eyes away from him, not wanting him to read anything there. He was too damned smart for his own good . . . and for her peace of mind, she thought wryly, edging closer to the bedside.

Price stood up and looked down at her, his green eyes probing. "Take your shower, Lee. I'll have Gladdy call Doctor Spellman." He inclined his head, a half-smile on his face, then left the room.

Lee felt strangely disoriented. Would she never be free of this helpless feeling when Price was near her?

She let the hot water needle her body as she scrubbed hard with the loofah sponge. Then she shampooed her hair, groaning when she touched a tender spot. When she was finished, she wrapped a towel, sarong-fashion, around herself, then swathed her head with another one. Although the fan had cleared most of the steam from the room, the vanity mirror still needed some wiping. She gasped, horrified, when she got a clear image of herself in the mirror. The right side of her face was a yellow and blue mask right to the hairline. She looked as though she had had all her teeth extracted on one side.

She was still staring into the bathroom mirror when Price returned. He laughed when he saw her open-mouthed reaction to her reflection.

"You look like you lost the title, darling," he drawled, his eyes amused.

"You should see the other guy," Lee responded like an

automaton, not looking away from the mirror. "Price, I can't go out of the house looking like this."

He leaned over, removing her hand from her face and kissing the bruise. "We have an appointment with Doctor Spellman in one hour at the hospital. Shall I dress you?" His eyes narrowed on her, watching the embarrassed flutter of her hands, then lifted to hold her eyes in the mirror. He was standing close to her, his body grazing her back. In slow motion he reached around her and with one quick touch loosened the towel. His hands replaced it where it dropped from her breasts. Try as she might, she couldn't look away from his image in the mirror. Her breathing was labored as she felt his heart thudding into her back. She closed her eyes and leaned back against him, incapable of pushing him away. She heard him kick the door shut.

"Darling? I have to love you. Tell me you want it. Lee?"

Without opening her eyes, she turned in his arms, her mouth finding his, her naked body pressed against him, as if her life depended on this physical contact.

"Mommy, Mommy? Are you in there? Gladdy says its time to eat," Rica called through the door.

Lee's eyes snapped open. She couldn't look at Price as she fumbled for a towel and called to Rica that she was coming.

Breakfast was an ordeal for Lee. Trying to find an explanation that was truthful but not too detailed that would satisfy Rica was a mind-bending endeavor. The little schoolgirl's saucer-eyed stare never left Lee all the while she drank her juice and had her slice of toast.

"I'm glad I waited to see you before I went to play with Johnny, Mommy. I never saw a face with so many colors before. Doesn't Mommy look funny, Daddy?"

"Yes." Price laughed, his eyes dancing when Lee glared at him.

When Rica finally skipped off to play, saying that she

was going to look for Johnny so that he could come and see her mommy, Gladdy looked questioningly at Lee.

To her relief, Price explained to Gladdy for her. Lee was glad to escape to her room on the pretext of getting her purse. She had no wish to hear what Price told the older woman.

The ride to the city was slow and traffic-filled since it was a market day. Wagons and trucks clogged the artery.

"What did you tell Gladdy, Price?"

"The truth. I even included your remark that it was an accident," Price said flatly, a little muscle jumping in his cheek.

"It was, Price."

"So you said." Price bit out the words. "Whatever it was, no man should ever hit or shove a woman and certainly not my wife."

"Price, please, you're not going to say anything to Grant about this, are you?" Lee pleaded. "I would rather forget it."

"Then forget it. I assure you I have no desire to discuss Lieber with you," Price said grimly, placing a cassette in the tape player. The voices of Barbra Streisand and Barry Gibb were a welcome intrusion.

A farm truck loaded with crates of squawking chickens wheeled by them, swaying precariously, going far too fast for good control.

"That damned lorry driver should be cited," Price muttered, his own hands loosely sure on the wheel.

"Not lorry, Price." Lee smiled at him. "Truck."

"What?" He frowned, not taking his eyes off the road. Then he laughed. "Oh. Right. Don't worry, Lee, I'll sound like a native New Yorker in no time," he said, his sudden imitation of a Yankee twang sounding authentic.

"Never." She let her head fall back against the seat. "You could never rid yourself of those lovely clipped Oxford accents. Besides, I like the way you speak. I find that Rica imitates many of your speech intonations. Sometimes she does it too well. Gladdy says she told Johnny that Willie Covert was a dumb blighter."

"She didn't!" Price hooted. "I don't use that word. Do I? Lord, I'll have to watch myself."

Lee nodded, closing her eyes.

"Pain, darling?"

"Just a little car sick, I guess. I'll be fine, Price."

"Try to sleep, if you can. I think I know the way from here on."

Lee must have dozed. The next thing she knew, Price was shaking her gently and calling her name. It took her a few moments to waken fully but she refused to let Price carry her, preferring to wait until she was fully awake and then making her own way, holding tight to Price's arm.

Dr. Spellman was friendly but professional as he questioned Lee about her face and head. He concluded after his examination that she had suffered a mild concussion. He assured her that the swelling and the soreness would disappear in a matter of days. "I had a tough time keeping that husband of yours from accompanying us into the examining room. Is he always so bent on getting his own way?"

"Yes. Always." Lee smiled, noting the way the doctor was watching her.

"Then I take it, by your smile, that you and your husband are not having troubles?"

Lee stared at the doctor dumbfounded, realizing that he could have thought Price had done this to her. "No, doctor, no, Price Chatham would never hit a woman. He just isn't like that."

"Good. I was just wondering what put that grim look on his face. He looks like he's been chewing bullets," Dr. Spellman said dryly, tying up the hospital gown Lee had on. "Come along. You can dress now."

A nurse put her head around the door of the dressing

room and informed Lee that her husband would return shortly and would she like some coffee.

"Oh? Yes, coffee would be nice. Did my husband say where he was going, nurse?"

"No, Mrs. Chatham, just that he would return shortly."

Lee nodded her thanks and finished dressing. She was sitting in the cafeteria when Price returned. He was approaching her table with Dr. Spellman, who at Price's urging joined them for coffee. When Price returned to their table with a fresh pot of coffee and three cups, Dr. Spellman frowned at his hands.

"How did you skin your knuckles, Mr. Chatham?" Not bothering to pay attention to Price's offhand answer, he signaled to one of the nurses, who said that she would be glad to put some ointment on the grazes.

It amused Lee to watch the doctor and the nurse maneuver Price into a small room after he finished his coffee.

When they were walking out to the parking lot, Lee looked at his hands again. "Were you working on the car, Price? Your hands look sore."

"They aren't sore. Besides, I'm a fast healer. Are you tired, Lee?" Price quizzed her, settling her on the seat.

"No, not tired, just a little sleepy, relaxed."

"I think the trip to New York will be good for both of us. You need a change of scenery. I need to have you alone for a while." He stared at her, watching her reaction to his words.

A faint pique edged her mind at his ability to read her so easily. Deliberately she let her lashes drop over her eyes, unwilling to let him have his way. She thought of his abraded knuckles again. "Were you changing a flat tire? What were you doing, Price? I never knew you to work on a car," she stated, pointing to his hands.

"Um? What? Oh, those. Most things you do on a car are hard on the hands. I can remember when I was driving Formula Ones. That was before we met. Well, anyway, I did much of the mechanic work myself. My hands were bruised and torn most of the time. Jesse, my mechanic, allowed me to work right along with him. I learned a great deal. I remember once when we were in France . . ."

Lee listened in a half-doze, registering that she hadn't known that Price had raced, wondering how much about him she didn't know. In a vague way she was aware that Price hadn't answered her questions about his hands.

When they reached home, she went straight to bed. She heard Price say he was taking Rica to the beach before she fell into a deep sleep.

"Lee? Lee? You've been asleep for two hours. I want to speak to you before Price and Rica return." Gladdy took a deep breath and sat on the bed as Lee struggled to sit upright. She was biting her lip as though trying not to laugh. "It seems your husband took umbrage at his wife's swollen face."

"What do you mean?" Lee yawned.

"It seems he made an appointment with the counselor while you were in the hospital."

"What counselor? What are you talking about, Gladdy?"

"I'm telling you that Ada Pierson called . . ."

"Grant's secretary?" Lee floundered.

"Will you let me finish! Yes, Grant's secretary. She called me to tell me that Price said he was coming into the office with or without an appointment . . . so Ada gave him an appointment." Gladdy stopped talking, a giggle stifling her voice. "He socked Grant in the chin, Ada said, and told him if he ever came near his wife again he'd get more of the same."

"No," Lee said faintly. "He wouldn't do that. Price doesn't lose his temper. He's controlled."

Gladdy laughed dryly. "It seems to me that you make a habit of underestimating that husband of yours, Lee."

"Grant will sue him," Lee gasped.

"I don't think so," Gladdy said, her eyes alight. "I don't think so at all."

"Gladdy . . . Gladdy, I don't know how to handle this."

"Don't worry, Lee," Gladdy chortled. "I think you have a man who knows how to handle anything."

CHAPTER FIVE

The plane trip to New York from the Rochester Airport was only an hour. Lee decided to sleep, finding it easier than making conversation with Price, who had retreated into one of his black moods. Sleep wouldn't come. Instead, her mind filled to overflowing with thoughts she'd rather not have. She found herself remembering the moments after Gladdy had informed her of Price's altercation with Grant. *Altercation, hell!* Lee thought grimly to herself. It was a punch out. She lifted her hand to the right side of her face, noticing a slight tenderness even yet.

When Gladdy had left her room that day, Lee had gone into the bathroom to take a shower. She had shampooed with caution, finding much of her head and face sensitive and sore, her jaw quite swollen. She had closed her eyes facing up into the spray, gasping at the coldness of the final body rinse she was giving herself.

She felt a feather touch at one breast. Stepping back from the water, she wiped her eyes. "Price! What are you doing here?"

"Joining you. Rica is out in the kitchen with Gladdy eating biscuits before they take some fresh bread to Mrs. Klem. She is under the weather with sciatica, I understand. We'll be alone in the house in a matter of minutes," Price said, stepping closer to her, his hands reaching for her. "Ouch, that water's cold. Hmmmm, but you feel nice and warm and soft."

Lee flicked quick, secret looks at his body, feeling the

heat in herself. She cursed the languor that was overcoming her as she looked at him through the curtain of her lashes. He wasn't aware of her watching him. His gaze was fixed on her own body. Lee stared at the strong, grave face, the prominent Greek cheekbones, the wide, high, intelligent forehead, the heavy-lidded emerald eyes fringed with those ridiculously long, thick lashes, the slightly hooked nose, the firm but sensual mouth. It was all as familiar to her as her own features . . . more so. When she had been living with Price, she had spent hours tracing his features with her fingers, touching his body everywhere with an indescribable sensual pleasure. Still, never had her fascination for her husband's body been as intense as it was at this moment.

She lifted her eyes to his face to find him watching her, reading her again. "Uh, if you'd like to wash, I'll leave you to it. I've finished," Lee gulped.

"Have you, darling?" Price's eyebrow arched, his voice humorous and satirical. "How disappointed you'd be if I accepted that statement as fact."

"What is that supposed to mean?" Lee flared. "Trying to be clever, are you?"

"You know what it means, Lee," Price said, one finger touching her nipple. "Clever has nothing do with it. I just know you."

"You think you do," Lee gasped, pressing against the wall of the shower. "I'll thank you not to practice your amateur psychology on me. Take a trip through someone else's mind for a change!" she snapped, turning her face away as he bent nearer, his one hand splaying on her abdomen in a slow counter-clockwise motion. She bit her lip on a moan, closing her eyes against the weakness invading her limbs.

She didn't demur when he switched off the shower and began to towel her. Sighing, she wrapped her arms around his neck when he lifted her into his arms. His mouth fastened to hers and she began to tremble, her hands digging into his shoulders, yielding to him. His firm mouth parted hers and she felt his tongue probe hers in gentle persuasion. She felt giddy with excitement as his mouth fed hungrily on hers. Lee felt him press her down into the softness of the bed and she pulled him to her.

"Tell me you want me, Lee. Tell me," he grated, his voice ragged.

She felt her body throb into accelerated heat at his words, her hands caressing him in urgent demand. "Price . . . yes." Her voice palpitated in her ears like a stranger's.

His mouth and hands touched her everywhere. Her body came to life with an almost painful heat as he urged her on to greater feeling and response. The parts of her that she had stored away in a tight airless container broke through as his hands and mouth released them. She heard someone cry out and realized through a haze that it was her own voice. There was a ringing in her ears and a glaze over her eyes but she had never felt sharper or more in tune with life. The nagging, mounting need spilled over them both, lifting and spinning them into one. She felt herself taken, her response rising to his, her cries bitten into his shoulder. Her mind cried "I love you, Price, I love you, Price," until she was sure she had said it aloud.

Later, as she lay quietly against his shoulder, his kisses still touching her hair and face, she looked up at him, her smile flickering in sudden shyness at the blatant, possessive glitter in his eyes. She caught at his hand as it stroked down her face, feeling the abraded skin on his knuckles. "That was some car that bruised your fingers," she said pointedly, her erratic breathing stilling slowly.

Price was still, his eyes fixed on her as he sorted out her meaning. "Who told you? Was it Gladdy?" His finger marked a soft path down her cheek.

"Yes. Grant's secretary is her friend. Why didn't you tell me?"

Price shrugged, leaning back from her. "It didn't seem important that you know. It was important that Lieber know that no man strikes my wife. I'll not have you mauled." Price bit the words off, placing a finger on her lips when she was about to speak. "And don't bother telling me it was an accident again. He should have made no moves on you at all. No one is going to do that to you, no one. Now let's forget it."

Lee looked at the hard sheen of those emerald eyes and felt a stab of pity for Grant. Still, could she deny the warm, protected feeling that filled her?

As Price rolled out of bed to his feet and stretched, Lee's eyes roved over his well-proportioned body. He was a Greek god, for sure. The thought made her smile. Price smiled back at her.

"I hope you like my body as much as I like yours, lovely wife. I don't think I'll ever tire of looking at you, or making love to you." He grinned wickedly as she reddened. "My, my, love, you do blush all over," he drawled, reaching for his terry robe and heading for the shower.

The moment he left the room, she felt a sense of loss. She shook her head and sighed, forcing herself not to think of the future when he was gone from her. A man like Price would never settle down with one woman. Felice Harvey had proved that.

She rose from the bed, not bothering to put on her wrapper before making the bed. She looked at herself in the full-length mirror, at her flat stomach, narrow waist, round breasts, slim legs. She was tiny but well-proportioned, she assured herself, patting her flat stomach absentmindedly. All at once she stiffened. She had taken no precautions last night. Don't be silly, she told her open-mouthed image, you won't get pregnant. She pressed her fist to her mouth, wondering.

The rest of the week, she had avoided Price, not able to explain to him that she was afraid of getting involved with him again only to have him leave her. His puzzlement turned to irritation, then to a cold anger that caused him to begin ignoring her. By the time they had packed and were ready to leave to catch the plane to New York a cold war existed between them. For Rica's sake they presented a united front at departure time. Rica was not unhappy at being left behind, knowing that she and Gladdy would be joining them in three weeks time in New York. Then the four of them would be going to England to see Frederick.

Lee looked out the airplane window at the layers of cotton clouds beneath them. Shortly they would be in New York, at La Guardia Airport, and she and Price had not exchanged a single word. She turned toward him, clearing her throat. "It seems foolish of me to travel with you to New York if we're not going to talk. I could have stayed behind and come to the city with Gladdy and Rica."

He turned those quartz eyes on her, his mouth a sardonic twist. "You'd like that, wouldn't you, Lee? If I left you behind? Not a chance, lady. You'll stay under my eye from now on." He shifted deeper into his seat, his eyes closing. It startled Lee when he continued speaking. "No way are you getting away from me again. Besides, the business is half yours. You can come along to all the business conferences and watch the wheeling and dealing during the merger."

"I'm sure you do that very well. Wheeling and dealing, I mean," Lee snapped, hunching her shoulder.

His laugh was dry, without humor. "Very well, indeed. Perhaps if I had relied on cold business logic six years ago and not emotion I would have avoided a very painful ordeal and had my wife and child at my side where they belonged." He turned his head to look at her. "Aren't you interested in seeing Apple House become part of Chatham and Inglis? You should be. You have a vested interest in both sides."

Lee shrugged. "Yes, I'm interested in the merger from that standpoint, but I also know that my knowledge of the publishing business is not up to date."

"So? You'll learn again," Price said dryly, trying to

smother a yawn. "I'm going to take a catnap. We have about fifteen minutes until touchdown."

Price eased them through the airport hassle with minimum fuss, and soon they were in a cab racing for Manhattan. Even at the breakneck speed the cabby was maintaining, to Lee the ride seemed longer and more fraught with tension than the plane ride.

"Are . . . are we staying at the Grand Hyatt?" Lee queried, clutching at the seat as she slid sideways toward Price.

"No," he said coldly. "Frederick and I maintain a flat here in New York, overlooking Central Park." He was watching her again, that computer mind tallying her discomfort, recording her feelings. He pulled her close to his side, clamping her tight against any maneuver the taxi could make. He was making her safe from physical hurt but his aloof manner was wounding her another way.

While Price paid the cab driver, Lee stood back to admire the concrete facade of the apartment building they had stopped at, with its balconies winging out to capture the view of Central Park. It had a more modern look than the London flat had, but there was the same aura of subdued elegance. *How typical of Price to want the best,* she thought, wryly amused.

"Can I share the joke or is it private?" Price asked blandly as he gestured to her to precede him to the elevator. Price thanked the doorman for his help, then they were speeding to their floor. The elevator opened directly into the foyer of the apartment. The phone rang as Price was shutting the door, so Lee was spared from answering his question, and Price seemed to have forgotten it as he turned, frowning, from the phone. "That was Nick, Nick Petrus. Do you remember meeting him?"

"Yes, of course, we met when you were in the hospital here."

He shot her a cool assessing look. "Of course. You

signed for my treatment but didn't bother to stop and see how I was doing. How could I forget you, Florence Nightingale?"

"Your room was a bit crowded that day. I didn't want to break up your tête-à-tête with the queen of the soaps," Lee snapped.

"Jealous, darling?" Price crooned. "You don't seem to be able to handle any of the more mature emotions, do you?"

Before she could do more than sputter, he had wheeled toward the bedroom, saying he had to go out for a while and he was sure she could find something to amuse her while he was gone.

Lee ground her teeth. She was glad there were two bathrooms in their bedroom suite. She found a robe and locked herself in one of the bathrooms for a long relaxing bath. She heard the outer door slam and expelled a breath in relief. At least she would have a few hours free of him.

She was brushing her hair in front of the vanity mirror when the phone rang. She lifted the bedroom extension. "Hello?"

"Lee? Is that you, Lee? Did you just get in?" Alma's smoker's cough interrupted her string of questions. "I called the farm and your friend Gladdy said you were coming to town. I have good news. Tom Brewster called me. They want to talk about making *Lace Curtain Summer* into a movie for TV. They'd like to meet with you, if possible." Alma inhaled, and Lee could almost hear the smoke entering her lungs. "You . . . uh . . . remember Steve Blaylock? You met him at my party in June? Yes, that's the one. Well, it seems you made quite an impression on Steve and he's been touting you to the TV people. I'm not saying that's why these people want the book, but it doesn't hurt to have someone like Steve pulling for you." Alma cleared her throat. "Of course, I don't know how Price will like it . . ."

"When would they like to meet with me, Alma? I can

make it almost any time in the next two weeks. After that we'll be going to England to see Frederick," Lee said, grateful that she would have something to fill in the time when Price would be away from the apartment.

"Good. I'll set something up for tomorrow or the next day and get back to you right away," Alma said brusquely.

While waiting for Alma's call she decided to explore the apartment. The gleaming chrome and black kitchen drew her like a magnet. She couldn't help wondering who used the ultramodern room with its myriad assortment of utensils and appliances. She was still poking in and out of cupboards when Alma called back.

"Lee? We have an appointment with Tom tomorrow. I rang Steve and told him and he said that he would meet us there. It looks good . . . knock on wood," Alma said superstitiously. "You know, Lee," Alma stated, her voice tone changing. "If I had known you and Price were coming to town tonight, I would have gotten you tickets. We're going to see a play at the Brooks Atkinson theater. I think you would have enjoyed it."

"Oh, thanks, Alma. That sounds good, but don't worry about us. We might just stay in tonight. I don't know what Price's plans are." *No truer words were ever spoken,* Lee thought, as she replaced the phone on the cradle. *I have no idea what that man is planning any time,* she grated to herself. Well, he had better not plan her life for her, she thought bitterly, because she was going to do a few things that she wanted to do while she was in New York.

She wandered back to the bedroom and looked around her again. In a corner under a window she saw a typewriter that she hadn't noticed before, a modern electric with all the latest features. She sat down in front of it and switched it to on, then tentatively began to type. It was so easy! She went to her suitcase and removed the manuscript of her half-finished novel, *Amanda.* Her work was erratic at first, but gradually, as she fell into a rhythm, the flow of words began increasing.

She had no sense of the passage of time, but knew she must have been working a couple of hours. She sighed, switched off the machine, and leaned back, putting her right hand to the back of her neck to massage away the stiffness.

Suddenly the hands at her neck were not hers. She felt herself eased back until her head was resting against Price, his hands rubbing warmth into her shoulders and neck.

"Tired, Lee? You should have rested this afternoon." He reached for her, lifting her and carrying her to a wing-back chair in one corner of the bedroom. He sat down with her in his lap, one hand stroking her neck as he cradled her with the other. She could feel a quivering in her abdomen, a weakness in her limbs. She looked at him in helpless excitement as his probing hands became more insistent. He watched her, his green eyes enigmatic, alert. He pushed back the edge of her robe exposing a white shoulder and the half-moon cleft of one breast. He let one finger stroke her breast, his eyes roving her face as though each part of her gave him the message he wanted. His finger was now under her jaw, tracing her jawbone in a feather touch that made her mouth dry and swallowing difficult. "Relax, darling, I'm not going to hurt you." He watched her, still, his green eyes cool and assessing.

Oh, yes, you are, Lee agonized mutely, *you're going to take me apart piece by piece if I don't watch you every second.* She let her body sag against him, fatalistic about the instant rise in heat that filled her. "What . . . what are we doing tonight?"

"Oh, I thought we might take in a show. I picked up some tickets at the office this afternoon. Then there's a party, if you'd like to go. I thought it might be relaxing to dine here, then go on to the show. Unless you'd prefer to eat out . . ." Price shrugged, his hand sliding down her neck to the opening of her robe. His eyes, which had been fixed to hers, suddenly dropped to watch his hand. She could feel his breathing quicken near her cheek. Without those eyes manacling her she was able to force herself to break free of him. He felt her trying to struggle upward and his hand closed over her breast. "Where do you think you're going?"

"We really don't have much time if you want to make the theater on time," Lee mumbled, as she eased herself off his lap. He released her at once, making no effort to hide his arousal as she stood. She tore her gaze from his mocking one and was almost to the door before he spoke.

"Run away, this time, Lee, but don't think it will happen that way every time. It won't."

She stood there for a moment, her back to him, angry words running through her mind. She bit her lip and left him still sprawled in the chair.

They dined in relative silence, the muted music of the stereo sounding clear and distinct.

"Are we going to the Brooks Atkinson theater?" Lee asked, taking a sip of her Chablis, making ineffectual pushes with her fork at the sole almandine that had been prepared by Price's maid.

"No," Price said tersely. Then he gave her a sharp look. "Why do you ask?"

"Alma called when you were out. She said that she and her party were going there. I just thought perhaps that's where we were going." She shrugged.

"We're going to the Eugene O'Neill."

"Oh."

The cab ride to the theater was a repeat of the dinner . . . silent. Lee was prepared to hate the evening and fumed in silence at Price's continued quietness. "You must be a hit with your dates if you show the same sparkling wit with them as you're doing with me," she snapped.

"I've had no complaints so far." Price eyed her mockingly.

"I'll bet you haven't," Lee hissed, wishing she had not brought up the subject.

"If you're fishing in order to find out whom I've been taking around . . ." he began smoothly.

"I'm not," Lee interrupted, her voice hoarse. "I have not the slightest interest in your sordid little affairs," she lied.

"They weren't sordid. Diverting, intriguing, stimulating . . . yes, but sordid? No, not that. Shall I tell you about them so that you can judge for yourself?" he goaded.

"Don't be ridiculous!" Lee grated, glad when the cab pulled to the curb and they could alight and mix with the crowd entering the theater.

The play was delightful, and Lee was able to forget Price for a short time. During the intermission they were still silent with each other. Though Price nodded to a few people, he made no effort to join anyone.

After the play, Price was able to find a cab, though others were having trouble. He explained to Lee that he had paid the driver a fee to pick them up at curtain time.

The ride to a brownstone on a tree-shaded street, where the party was being held, was short. Intrigued, Lee studied the other row houses along the way while Price took care of the taxi.

"Like them?" Price whispered quite close to her ear.

"Yes, I do." Lee nodded, turning her head slowly, admiring the electric lights in the shape of gas lamps. "I knew such places existed in Manhattan, but I've rarely seen as nice a neighborhood as this one."

Price shepherded her up the stairs to the old-fashioned front door recessed in the brick wall. Instead of ringing the bell, he turned the handle and stepped into a small foyer that opened directly into a large room filled with people, pushing, laughing, drinking, and chatting over the sound of a piano playing honky-tonk music.

"Well, darling, you did come . . . and you brought . . . oh, dear, I'm so poor with names."

"Hello, Darvi. How are you?" Price asked, bending to kiss the pouting mouth of Darvi Lindquist. "This is my wife, Lee. Her professional name is Rennie Gilbert. Darling, you remember Darvi, don't you?"

Lee felt Price's hand tighten on her arm as she tried to move away from him. Her tongue felt cloven to the roof of her mouth. *Damn his soul,* she cursed him silently, *for bringing me here.* Her eyes lifted to the cold-eyed stare of the colorful Darvi, her artificial smile echoed by her own, Lee was sure. "Yes, we met at Alma's party last June."

"So we did," Darvi said in a bored tone before turning toward Price. "Do come with me, darling, and tell Clint how to make those delicious Peach Fuzzes that you make."

"It will be a pleasure. Come along, darling. You'd probably like a cool drink," Price coaxed, putting his arm around Lee and pulling her with him, much to the chagrin of the lovely Darvi.

"No, you go ahead," Lee stated, her lips tight. "I'll follow along in a moment."

Price stared at her for long seconds, his eyes probing her thoughts and separating them. He gave a slight nod that was almost a shrug, then followed Darvi, greeting other acquaintances on his way.

He's well liked, Lee mused, as she watched him cross the room. People gravitate to him, listen when he speaks. Clever, witty Price reading people like others do the daily papers, cataloguing them and filing them but never revealing himself. She gave a shiver as she thought of his mind turned upon her.

"Hello, Rennie Gilbert. I've missed you . . . very much."

Startled, Lee turned to see Steve Blaylock smiling at her, offering her one of the drinks in his hand.

"White wine," he said. "Not a Riesling, but a nice, soft white just the same. I took a sip. Do you mind?" He grinned, as one brow lifted impishly.

"No." Lee laughed. "I don't mind. I'm flattered that you remember what I prefer to drink."

"Oh, I remember a great deal more than that, but I'd rather discuss that in a more private place than Darvi Lindquist's living room."

Startled by the suggestive warmth in his voice, Lee's eyes flew to his face. She tried to mask her blush by sipping the wine. "Alma tells me that we have a meeting scheduled for tomorrow with Tom Brewster about *Lace Curtain Summer.* I understand I have you to thank for supporting the book when you talked to Tom. Thank you."

"Don't think for one moment if *Lace* wasn't good that I would push it. I wouldn't," Steve said dryly. "You may have knocked me off my pins little lady, but you didn't jar my brains."

Lee's bubble of laughter escaped her on an exhaled breath, causing some of the people nearby to look around and smile. She didn't demur when Steve took her arm and led her to a small loveseat near the floor-to-ceiling window, where a large potted plant gave a measure of privacy from the other guests.

"So, tiny lady, tell me why you haven't been to town until now." Steve lifted a hand, palm outward, at her look of surprise. "I know because I've been calling Alma to see when you would be coming. Have you had a busy summer?" he said softly, leaning toward her on the settee.

Lee thought of all the upsets and upheavals at Highland Farms and nodded, her smile rueful.

"Alma flattened me when she said that you were married to Price Chatham," Steve stated, staring at his drink, swirling the contents in a slow, measured way. "I've never had worse news." He looked up at her, his face still, watching her.

"Steve, I can't . . ." Lee began, reaching out a hand to touch the hand that lay on his leg, not wanting to hurt him.

"Pardon me," Price said through his teeth, menace in every line of him. The man who controlled a publishing empire with verve and panache had disappeared. Lee's heart thudded in slow cadence at the aura of danger. Price's eyes pierced her face then followed an imaginary line downward to her hand, his gaze fixed in close observation at the way the two of them sat, close, touching. A muscle jumped in his cheek, and his right shoulder flexed in a restless way.

Taut, unsure of herself, Lee rose, not looking at either man. "Are we leaving, Price?" she asked, the sound of her voice alien to her.

"Yes."

Lee rose, her arm quickly gripped by Price. "Good night, Steve. It was nice seeing you again."

"It was nice seeing you, Rennie. Price." Blaylock's lips tightened when Price ignored him.

It seemed to Lee that Price swept her through the room. It galled her that with all his rush, he took the time to make his farewells to Darvi Lindquist.

A soft summer rain was freshening the air as they descended the outside steps to the sidewalk and a waiting cab. They settled themselves against either side of the vehicle in silence.

"I didn't realize you were so intimate with Blaylock," Price said, his face rigid.

"Don't be a fool!" Lee lashed back, hating his controlled anger. "I met Steve at Alma's party in June . . . not that it's any of your business."

"Oh, I think it's my business," he responded silkily, his voice reminding her of a velvet-covered knife. "You're my wife, Lee. I won't have you trying it with another man . . ."

"Of all the pompous, insufferable hypocrites . . ." she sputtered, furious enough to strike him. "You carry on with everything in skirts but you expect me to be Caesar's wife."

"Don't try to pin any labels on me, lady. Yes, I had women . . . after you ran out on me . . ."

"And during our marriage . . ."

"After you ran out on me is what I said and what I mean. There was no one but you after we married . . . and I don't carry on with everything in skirts. What the hell, Lee! Did you expect me to turn my collar around just because you didn't want me? I'm a normal male and I had women . . ."

"Oh, I'm damn sure of that," Lee hissed at him.

"Stop trying to make me something I'm not. Just remember that you're my wife. I won't have you encouraging anyone. Don't forget that."

"And don't you forget that I intend to live my own life, not subject to your likes and dislikes. You remember that."

"We'll see." Price turned his face to look out the window.

While he paid off the cab, Lee walked into the apartment foyer. Courtesy dictated that she wait for Price, but Lee quietly damned good manners and stepped into the waiting elevator, punching the button to carry her upward. Before the doors closed upon her, her gaze was caught by Price's narrow-eyed stare as he came into the entranceway. Then she was alone, speeding up to her floor.

In her bedroom she stripped off her clothes, grabbed for her robe, and rushed to the shower just as the click of the outer door signaled Price's entrance. Locking the bathroom door, she turned the water on full strength to drown out any sound. She didn't want to speak to Price. She wanted to claw at him for causing her this pain. Why had she mentioned his women? What masochistic flaw had caused her to open that can of worms? If she had thought of it all, she would have known that Price had had women. He was too virile a man, too passionate a man, to live without sex. Why did it bother her? Why couldn't she keep a casual facade with him?

How do you remain casual with someone you love, stupid? a wry voice inside her spoke out.

She groaned into her soap-lathered hands. Oh, God, how could she be so stupid! Somehow she had to get over him. She could never live with him as his wife, knowing that he didn't love her, knowing that he would pursue any woman who sparked his fancy. And there would be plenty of them, she was sure. Women flocked to Price. She rinsed herself with icy cold water.

There was ominous quiet from Price's bedroom as Lee emerged into her own room, donning a silky wrap. She thought it might help to read one of the many paperbacks that were on the nightstand, but when she had read the same sentence over five times, she sighed and put the book aside. Switching off the light seemed to switch on her brain. Try as she would she couldn't dispel thoughts of Price and the hordes of women she was sure he was connected with.

The digital clock on the night table said three-fifteen when she moaned and rolled over, her eyes slowly closing.

She awoke heavy-eyed, disoriented, her eyes roving the strange room with a disinterested scrutiny. She looked at the clock and jackknifed into a sitting position. She had less than an hour before she was to meet with Alma and Steve. She contented herself with a quick cold shower, hoping it would partly reduce the puffiness under her eyes. Then she tried to disguise the ravages of a sleepless night with her makeup.

She had decided to be aloof with Price, and was taken aback when the maid announced that Mr. Chatham had left quite early for his office. She breakfasted on juice, coffee, and a croissant delivered fresh from an uptown delicatessen, then dressed in a black cotton piqué summer suit with a cream-colored eyelet blouse. For accessories she chose a bone and black linen purse with matching sandals. She coiled her thick blond hair in a chignon at the back of her head, the stark style emphasizing her delicate facial structure and large blue eyes. She thought she looked the epitome of a proper businesswoman ready to face the day.

During the taxi ride to Alma's office, her thoughts were full of Price. *Perhaps I wouldn't be so jealous if I took a leaf from his book,* she thought. *Maybe I should take a lover to help me forget Price. It seems to work for him . . .*

"We're here, lady. Was there someplace else you wanted to go, 'cause if there isn't, I gotta . . ."

"Oh, no, this is where I want to be. Sorry, I was daydreaming . . ." Lee explained to the driver, tipping him too much.

Alma met her as the elevator door opened. "You're late. Tom Brewster may be an easygoing man . . . but he is also a busy one. What in hell have you and Price been doing, Lee? You look worn to your socks." As Alma said this she pushed open a door and spoke to a young woman seated behind a desk. In minutes they were led into a modern office done in black and chrome.

Steve Blaylock rose from a chair seated in front of a coffee table and walked toward her, leaning down to kiss her cheek. Lee allowed herself to lean on him, smiling up into his surprised face.

CHAPTER SIX

Tom Brewster was an amiable person to deal with, Lee thought, as long as you didn't forget you were also dealing with an extremely cool businessman. Lee leaned back in her chair, content to play the role of onlooker. Watching Alma deal with Steve and Tom was an education in itself. It didn't bother Lee one whit that she was only called upon now and then to answer a question on her manuscript, but she practically jumped out of her chair when Steve suggested she be advisory consultant on the TV script. While Lee was still shaking her head no Alma pounced on the idea, enthusiastically supporting it.

"Now, look, Alma, I don't think that I . . ." Lee began.

Alma waved her to silence. "Who is better qualified to decide on the direction of the script than the author herself?" Alma turned back to Brewster.

"We do have quite competent personnel to see to that, Alma," Tom informed her dryly. He went on to describe the creative approach they would be taking on the project.

Lee thought she was being dropped from Tom's consideration and slouched back in her chair, but she hadn't counted on Steve's high-pressure persuasion. To her surprise, she watched Tom begin to nod slowly, then agree to take her on.

"Oh, wait a minute. We'll be going to England soon," Lee argued. "I can't put that off. Rica will be joining us here in a few days. Then we'll be leaving. I will not cut short my visit to Frederick."

"You won't have to, Lee," Alma interrupted briskly. "Shooting won't begin until November. You'll be back by then," she finished, pushing a long, brown cigarette into her holder and lighting it with a satisfied air.

Lee looked helplessly at Steve, who nodded, his eyes warm, then at Tom, who shrugged in understanding. She had been commissioned.

They lunched at an intimate French restaurant, but Lee was scarcely aware of what she was eating. Try as she would, she couldn't imagine what Price would say when he heard that she would be spending a good part of the early winter in New York to act as consultant for a TV program. *Why, why, you fool,* she chided herself, *should you care what he thinks? I don't know why,* she answered herself, her fork piercing her herb omelette again and again.

"Not hungry, Lee?" Steve asked her softly, leaning over her.

"Uh, no, but the food is very good, isn't it?" She smiled at him blindly.

"Is it?" He laughed, reaching to untwine her fingers from the napkin that she was clutching in her lap like a lifeline.

"Well, how nice. I didn't know you were lunching downtown, Lee," Price said behind her chair, his green eyes narrowed and mocking.

Startled, Lee turned, upending the water glass near her plate, watching as the water dribbled onto her lap. Before she could move, Steve was wiping the spill with a napkin. When his hand went toward her lap, Lee felt herself lifted out of her chair.

"Here, Lee. Take my handkerchief. Perhaps you'll want to go to the powder room and dry yourself a little better. I'm afraid I uh . . . surprised you, didn't I, wife? Sorry, the fault is mine."

He doesn't sound sorry, Lee fumed to herself, shaking

her arm free of him. He sounds pleased with himself. She excused herself and moved away from the table.

"Wait, Lee, I'll come with you. Join us for dessert, Price," Alma announced breezily, grinding her cigarette into the ashtray and rising to follow Lee.

As the door to powder room closed behind Alma, Lee was already blotting much of the water mark from her suit. She continued the operation for long minutes, neither woman speaking.

"Well, what's wrong? Come on, Lee don't try to look innocent with me. You're boiling over about something. Is it because I pushed so hard for this consultant job for you? I know it can't be because Price spilled a little water on you. Lee? Lee, it isn't that, is it?" Alma asked, more than a little puzzled. "I thought that you and Price were all patched up. You are, aren't you?"

"No, we're not." Lee's head jerked up as she snapped the words out. "Oh, look, I don't mean to be rude . . . and I don't want to discuss my problems either, please. It's so complicated, I don't understand it myself."

Alma nodded slowly. "All right, Lee. I won't pretend that I understand. I don't, but I won't ask questions either. Just remember that if you want to talk, I'm here." Alma paused for a moment, looking into the large mirror and patting her hair. "It will work out on this consultant thing. You'll see. You'll like it. Come on, the skirt looks fine. I want to order the chocolate mousse they have here. I read an article in the *Times* not too long ago that said that you can eat anything you want and not gain as long as you eat it at noon and have a very small snacklike meal in the evening. Isn't that great?" She smiled at Lee impishly, patting at her generous hips.

Lee gave a reluctant laugh and followed her back to the table, feeling no desire for dessert whatsoever.

Price and Steve rose at the same time, but it was Price who guided her into her chair, then hitched his own close to it. "Coffee, darling? Or perhaps you'd like some champagne? They tell me that you are to be the consultant on the TV adaptation of your book. Are you planning to cut short our trip home to Stone Manor?" Price quizzed in silken tones.

"No," Lee hissed, lifting her coffee cup to her lips and taking too big a swallow of the scalding liquid. Gasping, she reached for her ice water, but it was too late to stop the burning of her mouth. Turning a fulminating gaze on her husband, she spoke hoarsely. "If you know about the job, you also know that I won't be starting until November. Besides, Frederick may wish to return here with us then and spend Christmas with Rica and me at Highland Farms." She looked away again, taking another sip of the ice water, letting it soothe her lips.

"That sounds like a nice plan for all of us," Price drawled, taking a long draft of hot black coffee. "Perhaps you'll all excuse me now. I should rejoin my own party. I'll see you this evening, darling." Before he rose, Price caught her around the neck, and turning her face to his, planted a hard kiss on her stinging lips.

Lee looked down at her plate, taking deep breaths to steady herself, fighting the ambivalence of anger and sexual arousal. To her relief the others continued talking, either not noticing her agitation or trying to overlook it. When she did look up, her eyes went to Steve, who was gazing at a table on his right. Lee knew without looking it must be Price's table. Steeling herself against temptation, she kept her eyes on Steve and didn't turn her head.

Steve glanced back at her, one eyebrow arched in amusement. "I must say, you have to give her A for effort."

Lee took a deep breath and turned her head slightly. Her peripheral vision showed her Darvi Lindquist sitting very close to Price. There were two other men at the table, but to Lee it looked very tête-à-tête with Price and Darvi. She looked back at Steve, giving him a weak smile. "Yes, I agree, that she deserves an A."

"I don't like to defend what I consider to be the opposition, but I will tell you, Lee, that Darvi has been actively pursuing your husband for some time now. She is a very determined lady."

"Poor dear, he's such a helpless man—giving up without a struggle, it would seem." Lee smiled sweetly at Steve.

His shout of laughter brought Price's head around. Lee leaned closer to Steve and patted his arm. "I need you around all the time to laugh at my jokes." She sat back, swallowing hard. "Do you think we might go. I think I'd like a little fresh air."

Alma and Tom were amenable to leaving, both of them seeming quite satisfied with the results of the lunch.

"Lee says that she would like some fresh air, and I could use some exercise after that lunch. Why don't you two hop a cab? Lee and I will walk a bit before I get her a taxi," Steve urged Alma and Tom.

Alma looked from Steve to Lee and back again, then shrugged and nodded. She said good-bye, telling Lee she would call her tomorrow.

Lee said a hurried good-bye to Tom because Steve was pulling her with him down the avenue.

"Whew! Alone at last." He leered at her, making Lee laugh. "I thought we'd never get rid of those two."

"Steve, you've a very high-handed way with you at times. Has anyone ever told you that?"

"Only my mother . . . and my teachers . . . and my brother . . . and . . ."

"Never mind." Lee held up her hand, palm outward. "I get the idea. Ah, look at that little park. It's quite pretty, isn't it?" Lee pointed across the busy street. She and Steve crossed, jaywalking but keeping a watch for the police.

For the next two hours, Steve took her on a mini-tour of Manhattan, finishing up in Rumpelmayer's.

He overrode all Lee's objections and bought her a hot fudge sundae. She was still objecting when the concoction was brought to her. When she discovered the hot fudge was really hot, she capitulated. It was well after three when they parted. Lee felt pleasantly tired from her afternoon. She blessed Steve for keeping her so diverted that she hadn't given a thought to Price for the entire time.

She dozed slightly in the cab and was jarred awake by the bored driver telling her that the meter was running. The size of the wad of chewing gum in his mouth awed her. Again she overtipped.

As she stepped from the elevator into the foyer of the apartment, the phone began ringing. She knew the maid would be gone now, so she ran to pick it up in the living room. She got to it on the fifth ring.

"Mommy, it's me! Rica! I'm home from Johnny's now, so Gladdy said that I could call you."

"Hello, love, how are you? I miss you very much and can't wait until you come on Saturday. . . . When I called this morning, Gladdy said that you had gone to take a riding lesson from Mr. Greenway. Did you enjoy it? Were you careful?"

"Ohhhhh, yes! And I had the biggest horse in the world. . . ."

Lee listened to Rica extol the virtues of her horse as compared to Johnny's horse. Step by step, Rica described every bit of the riding lesson. When Gladdy finally took the receiver, she told Lee that the phone bill would be ridiculous. Then she proceeded to tell her what time they would be arriving on Saturday and that they would take a cab from La Guardia and not to send a car. Rica had to get on the phone once more to tell her mother about the new kittens that had been born in the Greenways' barn. Could she have one, please? Lee could hear Gladdy groaning in the background and fended her daughter off by suggesting they wait until they come back from England before they adopt a kitten. She could hear Gladdy's heartfelt "Amen to that" as she was replacing the receiver.

Still laughing, Lee rose from the couch and turned to

find a grim-faced Price standing in the doorway watching her. Startled, she lifted her hand to her mouth, irritation lacing her. "Don't you get tired of sneaking up on people?" she snapped at him.

"I didn't sneak up on you, Lee," he barked back. "You were so busy laughing with your phone friend you didn't hear me. Who was it? Blaylock?"

"It was Rica, if you must know. If I had known you were standing there I would have let you talk to her."

There was an arrested look on his face that made Lee feel uneasy. He seemed to be studying her again, she thought angrily.

"Stop looking at me that way!"

"What way? Why are you so sensitive about the way I look at you? After all I am your husband . . . or have you forgotten?"

"I've forgotten nothing . . . nothing. You're my husband only until a divorce is finalized. You remember that."

"And you remember to keep Blaylock at arm's length."

Glaring at her, he ripped the tie from his neck. "I'm taking a shower. I'll be calling Rica later. I'll let you know when in case you want to speak to her again." He stalked out of the room.

Sighing, she retrieved his tie from the floor and went to take a bath, deciding to invite Alma over for the evening. She didn't relish being alone with Price while he was in this mood. She just wasn't up to another battle.

When she did call Alma, though, the answering service informed her that she was out for the evening.

Lord, Lee groaned, rubbing a hand across the bridge of her nose, *what will I do with him? It's like baby-sitting a panther.*

She decided to dress up for dinner, donning a black sleeveless silk dress, understated and sexy, hoping that Price would get the message and suggest they dine at a restaurant, or at least take in a nightclub.

When she left her room, she heard rattling sounds in the

kitchen. Her heart sank to her shoes as she stopped in the doorway. Price had a ruffled apron tied around his middle, a shocking pink covered with green and yellow daisies. It looked even more garish against his deep maroon cotton dress jeans and cream shirt.

He looked up from his work of tearing spinach leaves and gave her basic black a mocking scrutiny. "You might be a little overdressed for the barbecue I have planned for us, but don't change. You look lovely."

"Are . . . are we staying in? Have you invited someone over?" Lee stumbled over the words. "I thought we might see one of the big shows in town. I hate to miss things like that. I'm in New York so seldom." She swallowed and took a deep breath, placing her trembling fingers behind her back, lacing and unlacing them in quiet frustration. "We could always have the barbecue when Rica and Gladdy arrive."

"So we could." Price's voice was suavely agreeable as he continued adding ingredients to the teak bowl. "If you wish we'll have another of these evenings when they do arrive." He lifted a bowl of shelled hard-boiled eggs and handed it to her. "Slice these, will you? The slicer is there . . . on the counter." He smiled when she took the bowl. Then he reached into a drawer in the cupboard and took out another apron. "Sorry about the colors, but the maid loves bright things. You look very fetching in purple ruffles."

"Lavender," Lee answered in hollow tones, tying it around her.

"Pardon me?" Price glanced down at her inquiringly. "Looks pretty on you, whatever the name is. Just put the slices in that crystal dish, next to the crumbled bacon. Good."

Lee worked with her head down, her movements mechanical, her mind racing. "Perhaps we could go somewhere after we dine. . . ."

"I thought it would be nice if we gave the new stereo

equipment a trial. I had it installed the last time I was in New York, but I never did get a chance to try it. I met you then at Alma's party, when I was in the hospital . . ."

"Yes, yes, I recall, and I would love to remain home and listen to some music, but . . ."

"Good, so would I," he interrupted. "That's settled. Now, I think we should get the lobsters ready. The maid prepared them, so all I have to do is put them under the broiler. Don't they look good?"

"Yes. Price . . ."

"Ah, you're right, I've forgotten the wine. Ah, here we are, chilling in the fridge. A Chenin Blanc. Just what I ordered."

He steam-rollered her into the dining room to show her the table that had been set for them. When he pressed a drink into her hand, Lee took a sizable swallow and choked, her eyes watering.

"Easy, darling. That was straight gin with a twist of lemon. A little stronger than what you're used to, I think." Price looked properly sympathetic as he wiped the tears from her cheeks with a cocktail napkin.

"Why didn't . . . you . . . tell . . . me?" Lee coughed, her voice rasping. "You know damn well I never drink before I eat." She glared at him, wanting to douse him with the rest of the drink as she watched the amusement grow on his face.

"Would you like me to get you something else?"

"No, thank you." Lee lifted the glass and drained it, suppressing a shudder. "Perhaps the drink will drug my senses and I'll be able to last through the evening."

"A few more belts like those two and you won't last through dinner," Price stated dryly, taking the glass from her.

Lee wasn't fooled by his casual tone. She could tell he was furious at her last remark. It gave her a sense of achievement to have scored off him, however small the mark was. She lifted her chin and preceded him back to the kitchen, not feeling as steady as she should but holding herself in rigid control. She would die before giving him the satisfaction of seeing her stagger. It was much hotter in the kitchen than it had been previously and Lee was glad when the lobsters were ready. They carried them, along with the salads and French bread, to the dining table.

She hadn't realized how hungry she was until she bit into the first forkful of juicy lobster dripping with lemon butter. They ate in virtual silence, both content to listen to the dramatic strains of "Romeo and Juliet," piped from the living room through recessed speakers in the walls.

After they'd eaten, they adjourned to the living room for the coffee and brandy.

"I wish I had said no to the chocolate mousse," Lee grumbled as she pressed a hand to her waistline before reaching for the silver coffee pot.

Price laughed softly and pressed his hand to the spot where hers had been. "You have a long way to go before you have to worry, lady. You are still as dainty and trim as you were at fifteen."

Lee turned, the coffee swirling in the cup she handed to him. "How do you know that? You didn't know me when I was fifteen."

Price's eyebrow arched upward, giving his face the satanic look that Lee found most disturbing. "Yes I did. Your father brought you to visit the villa we leased one season on Corfu. I came in from sailing and you were flashing all over the tennis court with that young Greek who had attached himself to you . . ."

"Niko . . ."

". . . at the moment of your arrival and who didn't unglue himself until your departure," Price said slowly, his eyes narrowing in remembrance, his lip curling in disdain. "I couldn't believe that anyone could be stupid enough to play tennis in all that heat . . ."

"Thank you," Lee said frostily, cursing herself for letting his words offend her.

"And be cute, leggy, and sexy and still be a baby . . ." Price continued, his grin widening as he watched her color rise.

"You never noticed me at all," Lee accused, remembering the raw pain she'd felt when she'd tried to be where Price would see her and he'd never noticed her at all. He had never even spoken to her. "I assumed you didn't even know of my existence, since you never acknowledged it."

"Did it rankle, little love?"

"No, it did not," Lee snapped untruthfully. "It just surprises me that you should remember someone that you had totally ignored."

Price threw back his head and laughed. "If I had done what I wanted to do, you would have been shocked out of your adolescent mind, and my father and yours would have shot me."

A reluctant smile touched Lee's lips. "They were a little overprotective of me, weren't they?"

"No," Price stated, his voice firm. "They just knew me too well. I knew that they had seen me watching you . . . and they read my mind quite accurately." His grin had a lopsided, lazy look that set Lee's pulses racing. "You were a great temptation, Lolita. That's why I stayed out of your way . . ."

"You mean why you chased the overdeveloped ladies who plied the yacht trade through the Ionian Islands," Lee said over her shoulder as she stood and walked to the stereo and pretended to study the numerous albums there.

Price's laugh was low, reaching out to Lee and curling her toes. "Darling, I'm shocked. I knew you were precocious but I hadn't realized how up on things you were then."

"I often heard Father and Frederick talking about what Frederick referred to as your peccadilloes. I remember them describing one called Maria. I was walking up from the tennis court and they were sitting on the terrace. I was below them so they couldn't see me. After they described her breasts, I felt as though I should have gone back to my training bra," Lee said dryly. Just the thought of Price with such a woman gave her the feeling that she would like to empty the vase of carnations that sat on the coffee table over his head.

Price was grinning more than ever, his eyes closing for a moment. "Ah, yes, the lovely, well-endowed Maria. She was a treasure. How could I ever forget such an exquisite armful."

"I understand she had a lovely mustache." Lee smiled brightly.

Price gave a shout of laughter. "Never." He stood and ambled toward her. "Jealous, my love?"

"Not in the least," Lee lied. "I am sure it would be only natural for you to be drawn to Greek women. You're half-Greek yourself."

"So I am," Price drawled. "I find them attractive, yes, but I have never lost my head over any dark beauty as I have over one diminutive blonde with sky-blue eyes and a doll of a figure."

Lee could feel the saliva dry in her throat at his words, her arms and legs becoming wet noodles. She turned from him, reaching down toward the stereo, loath to let him see how much his words affected her. When he pulled her back against his hard body, she was boneless and unresisting.

"Have I told you that the little basic black you're wearing is very sexy? Do you have many more of those . . . er . . . house dresses?" Price growled in her ear, his hand flattening on her tummy in a slow circular motion.

Relaxing against him with a burble of laughter, Lee tried to still his hand roving her abdomen. "You know very well this isn't a house dress," she gasped, inordinately pleased that he found it attractive.

"No? Well, then, do me a favor and let it become one, will you? I would rather you didn't go any farther than our living room in it. Ummmmm, you smell so nice too . . ." He reached around in front of her to flip a switch on the stereo system. Slow, beautiful music seemed to surround them. "Dance with me, Lee," he said, rising.

She turned into his arms, her body fluid against his, both arms clasping around his neck. One of his arms was close around her shoulders, the other low on her spine, fitting her tight to his body. She had forgotten how tall he really was. She felt enveloped by him, comforted, protected. Like many big men, Price was an excellent dancer, moving lightly and effortlessly to the music. The song throbbed and promised eternal love and Lee had to restrain herself from blurting to Price how much she loved him. Shivering at her own vulnerability, she tried to push herself away from him but he wouldn't let her, locking his arms more tightly to her.

"Don't struggle, love, relax. Don't you like the music?" he crooned, lowering his head a bit more to nibble on her earlobe.

"Yes . . . no . . . usually. Perhaps I'm more tired than I realized from all that walking . . ."

"What walking?" Price quizzed silkily, his steps moving her evenly around the floor.

"Oh. Uh, on my return here from the luncheon meeting, I walked. It was so nice and fresh after the rain last night . . ."

"Alone?"

"Alone? Uh . . . no. Steve was kind enough to accompany me . . ."

"Was he now?" Price growled, his hand tightening on her hip.

"Yes," Lee squeaked, feeling the suppressed tension in the body pressed tight to hers. "Would you have wanted me to be alone on my walk?"

"No. I would have wanted you to wait until you were

with your husband before you took your walk." The vocalist on the record sobbed her tortured love and the silence stretched between them.

Price whirled her again, his muscular thighs brushing the silkiness of her dress and clinging there. His green eyes dissected her. Her hands trembled down from his neck as she tried to ease herself back from him, but Price wasn't cooperating. Instead his hold tightened even more, so that they moved as one.

"No, my love, don't move away. Don't you know by now that this is where you belong?"

"It's late," Lee croaked, her face lifting from his neck.

"So it is. Shall we continue in bed?"

Lee looked up to give him a scathing answer and was lost in his green eyes. *Damn him for the eight kinds of demon he is!* she thought, watching his hard mouth curve into a sensual magnet. There was warmth there, a lovely contour. *Mouths shouldn't be beautiful,* she stormed at him in mute rebellion.

His lips touched hers and she took fire at once, not a roaring blaze, just a consuming simmer that ate away her control and fused her to him.

When he lifted her high in his arms, his mouth was still locked to hers, her hands clenched on his shoulders.

CHAPTER SEVEN

Even after the arrival of Rica and Gladdy, Lee had the feeling that she couldn't escape Price. He was everywhere. He had even accompanied her to the last meeting she'd had with Tom Brewster. The questions he fired at Brewster were pointed and abrupt and, to Lee, bordered on the impertinent. She sat motionless in her seat waiting for the explosion she was sure would come. She was surprised when Tom Brewster didn't lose his temper or insist that she be removed as consultant, and marveled at his calmness when Price insisted that he would be with his wife each day on the set.

"I don't think that's necessary, Price," Alma wheezed, inhaling deeply on her cigarette. "Steve will be there most days and so will I. I don't see the need . . ."

"Whether you see the need or not, Alma, I'll be with my wife when she's on the set. That's final." Price's voice had been adamant, and when his eyes roved the circle of persons sitting in the office they challenged anyone to argue with him.

Lee had a fluttering feeling that she couldn't identify. She felt weak and unable to cope as she listened to Price. She didn't once look at Steve, even though several times she could feel his gaze on her.

She was glad when Price made their excuses about lunch, saying that they had to rush back and have lunch with their daughter.

"Since we will be leaving for England tomorrow, Lee

and I will say our good-byes to you now," Price announced in his abrupt way.

All at once, Lee felt angry. Where did he get off making her good-byes for her? Who told him he was running her life? She lifted her head to tell him just that, not caring that the others might hear, when he took an iron grip of her elbow and propelled her out of the office, down the corridor and into a just-opening elevator.

"Just what in hell . . ." Lee sputtered, turning to him and trying to jerk her arm free in one motion.

"Keep it down, Lee. We'll talk later," Price hissed, inclining his head toward the blonde in net stockings who was looking him over quite openly.

"No, we won't. We'll talk now," Lee hissed back, glaring at the blonde and trying to hitch closer to Price because the corpulent man on her left reeked of garlic.

The elevator door opened and they spilled into the lobby. Price gave a fleeting smile to the blonde and Lee ground her high heel into his instep. She listened to his groan with immense satisfaction, lifting her chin and sailing by the fat man and out onto the street.

"What in hell did you do that for?" Price quizzed silkily into her ear.

"I will not have you leering at women when I'm with you," she grated, suppressing the anger she felt at the thought of the swinging-hipped blonde.

To Lee's relief, Gladdy and Rica were already at the apartment when they returned. Amid the exuberant greetings, Lee and Price's angry silences with each other were overlooked. Dinner was a noisy, laughing affair as Rica talked nonstop about her dog Duke and how lonesome he was going to be without her, the barn kittens at the Greenways, and her own overwhelming ability as a horsewoman.

The flight to England was bumpy and long, but Rica was enthralled with it all. The stewards and stewardesses were unfailingly cheerful with her, often initiating games that delighted the little girl. Price chatted with Gladdy quite often and Lee had to fight a sense of betrayal as she listened to the older woman laugh in delight at something Price had said to her. He ignored Lee for the entire flight. Once when she was trying to interest a yawning Rica in a nap, he came over to them and scooped the little girl into his arms. To Lee's relief and chagrin, Rica was asleep in minutes, cuddled in her father's arms.

London was bathed in moist warm darkness as they taxied away from Heathrow. Rica was yawning and hungry. Gladdy was groggy with lack of sleep. Lee felt jumpy. Only Price seemed unruffled and for that Lee could have strangled him. His serenity struck her as the height of pomposity.

"We're going to stay at the flat tonight and drive down to Stone Manor tomorrow. Frederick will be meeting us there," Price announced as he settled Rica on his lap in the front seat. She was very taken with Mr. Chisholm, the uniformed chauffeur from Chatham and Inglis who was driving them.

"Do you have a suit like Mr. Chisholm, Daddy?" she piped, imitating with her lips the phlegmatic Chisholm twitch.

When Price shook his head no, Rica looked disappointed. At the flat, Price insisted that Gladdy and Lee take Rica and go up on the lift ahead of him. He promised that he and Chisholm could handle the luggage.

Lee shrugged and led Rica and Gladdy to the elevator that would take them to their floor. Before she could fit her key into the lock, the door was flung open and Frederick stood there. A thinner, more aged version than she remembered, Lee thought, but still the same warm, loving man that she remembered. As she watched, tears rolled down his cheeks and he opened his arms wide to her. With a sob she rushed forward, enclosing him in her arms as he embraced her.

"Oh, God, Lee, my darling child, how I've missed you." Frederick swallowed with an effort then eased her from him, his eyes searching her face. "There has not been a day when I didn't want you back with me."

"Oh, Frederick, I've missed you too," she gasped, trying to control her shaking voice. "I didn't think you would be here. I thought . . ." Lee felt a tugging at her skirt and looked down at Rica in a dazed way. "Oh, darling, this is your grandfather. Frederick, this is Rica, who is named after you."

Lee heard Gladdy sob next to her as a smiling Frederick put out his arms and bent toward the staring child. For long moments Rica held back, her wide green eyes studying the stranger. Then slowly her dimples appeared, her lips parting in a gaping smile.

"I lost my tooth. The tooth fairy left me a quarter. I bought Duke an ice cream." Rica rushed into speech, then stepped into the circle of Frederick's arms. He lifted her high, holding her lightly and scrutinizing every feature.

"You have your grandmother's Greek coloring," he whispered, his voice hoarse.

Lee nodded, unable to speak. She pulled Gladdy forward but the other woman held back, gesturing to Lee to wait.

The three adults and Rica were still standing there when Price and the chauffeur arrived with the luggage. Price's darting glances assessed the situation, his glance lingering on Lee's tear-stained cheeks. With a minimum of fuss he dispersed the luggage to a man with a Cockney accent, who had come from the kitchen as though on silent signal, and dispatched the chauffeur.

Not quite knowing how she reached there, Lee found herself in the lounge, sitting in a snow-white conversation pit, a glass of dry sherry in her hand.

"Frederick," Price said softly, bringing his father's reluctant attention to himself. "What do you think of our daughter?"

"She's lovely, as lovely as her mother was." Frederick smiled at Lee. "You know, Lee, the way she moves reminds me of you at that age."

"Did you know me at that age, Frederick?" she quizzed, feeling a twinge of déjà vu as she remembered Price speaking of her when she was fifteen.

"My dear child, I came to the hospital to visit your mother when she had you. Even though she and I were not close, I was anxious to see the child of my dearest friend and soon-to-be colleague at that time. You were born in a hospital on Long Island. I remember the drive from Manhattan was fraught with traffic, but you were worth the trip, wrinkled and red though you were." Frederick chuckled, cuddling Rica close to him. "Now, Gladdy, you must tell me all about these two girls of mine and how they have been doing."

Lee groaned when Gladdy took Frederick at his word and launched into a detailed account of their years at Highland Farms. To Lee's surprise and chagrin, Price did not leave while Gladdy was holding forth. Far from it, he began to question Gladdy, eliciting even more information from the eager woman. Any attempts that Lee made to change the subject were met by blank stares from Price and smiles from Frederick. She felt a strong sense of relief when dinner was announced.

Rica was jubilant to be eating at the table with the adults, and her childish laughter permeated the atmosphere. Both her father and her grandfather seemed to find everything she said and did of immense importance. *She'll be spoiled before she attends first grade,* Lee thought, a reluctant smile on her face as she watched her daughter describe her beloved Duke with arm gestures and flowery phrases.

Halfway through the meal it became obvious to the adults that Rica was flagging and needed her bed. Before Gladdy could say anything, Lee, brushing aside protests from the men, lifted Rica from her chair and swept from the room, saying she knew where Rica would be sleeping.

"Mommy, Grandpa has a nice face like Duke and his hands don't hurt me when he hugs me like Uncle Grant's used to . . ." Rica yawned, then smiled as her mother tucked her in bed.

Lee didn't see Price until he bent down next to her to kiss Rica good night. "You don't have to worry about Uncle Grant hugging you anymore, love. He won't be," Price said softly.

"Oh, I didn't mind too much," Rica mumbled, almost asleep.

Lee raised herself from the side of the bed, aware that Price hadn't moved. She reached to turn the light off, feeling the heat from his body. "She really cares for Frederick already," she said in a breathy voice.

"I heard her description of him, a nice face like Duke's," Price whispered, a thread of amusement in his voice as he eased the door shut.

"The ultimate compliment from Rica." Lee grinned, shaking her head.

"Are you going downstairs?"

"No." She shook her head, not meeting his eyes. "I think I'll retire. If you're going downstairs you might tell them I'm going to bed." Lee's smile fluttered and faded.

"I'll tell them." Price's hooded gaze was enigmatic, his face expressionless.

Lee could feel menace emanating from him and her restless eyes probed his face, trying to read his thoughts. When he turned away without another word, she exhaled in relief.

She pushed open her bedroom door, irritation lacing through her again as it had when Price had told her where she would be sleeping. This was Price's room. It had also been hers in the early days of their marriage. It was also the room where she had found Price embracing Felice Harvey. She wished she had been given the other bedroom connected to their bathroom that Price was now using, but she didn't want to explain why she didn't want the room so she had said nothing. Still, she would have slept better in the other room, she thought, biting her lip in frustration.

Surging anger at the bitter memory drove all thoughts of sleep from her mind. She undressed carelessly, deciding a warm shower would probably relax her.

As she washed, she tried to block the upsetting pictures of Felice and Price from her mind. She thought how good it would be to get to Stone Manor and see Scylla again. The horses! Of course, she would take Rica to the stables to see the handsome jumpers and hunters that Frederick kept. Even though Lee was an indifferent rider, she had the feeling that Rica would be like her father and grandfather and love to ride.

The night was long and filled with painful images. Even her momentary lapses into sleep were clouded with warlike pictures of Price and herself, their faces contorted with hatred, their mouths agape as they shouted at one another. She surfaced once, her body bathed in perspiration, her hair stringy and damp around her face. She sat up in a jerky motion to bury her face in her hands. How could she live like this? Price hated her for leaving him, despised her for denying him his daughter for so long. Now he intended to pay her back in full by humiliating her through her body, by making her succumb to his physical mastery of her. How horrible it would be if he ever discovered that she loved him! It would be the most powerful weapon he could use against her.

When Lee entered the morning room the following day, she took a deep breath and pinned a smile to her face. To her relief, Price wasn't there but Gladdy and Frederick were, both smiling as Rica held forth on her beloved Duke.

Lee went to the sideboard and helped herself to some

buttered toast. She was pouring her coffee when the maid came in from the kitchen with a glass of frothy orange juice.

Frederick looked up at Lee and smiled, then gestured to the glass set before her place. "I hope that's the way you like it, my dear. As I recall, it was a cup of orange juice, a tablespoon of honey, and a raw egg whipped in a blender. Is that right?"

Lee felt a sudden prick of tears behind her eyes as she nodded. "Yes, Frederick, thank you." Swallowing, she tried to fight the rush of emotion that threatened to overcome her. "I'd . . . I'd forgotten how charming this room is. How lovely for Rica that she should have a sunny morning her first day in England." Lee looked away from Gladdy's narrowed gaze and glanced again at Frederick.

"I'm sorry, Lee, I meant to give you Price's message at once, but I was too busy hearing about Duke." Frederick gave her a rueful smile. "My son, as usual, has too many things to do at the office to drive to Stone Manor with us. He says that he'll be along in a day or so, for sure by the end of the week."

Lee felt a palpable relief flood through her at the thought of not having to see Price for a while. "Oh? Well, I know how busy the publishing business is," she said.

"That's right. You're an author now. I'm very proud of you, Lee." Frederick smiled at her again, making Lee feel warm and wanted. "Well, ladies, what do you say about getting ready for our journey now and we'll have a late lunch at Stone?"

Rica literally bounced with excitement at the thought of seeing the horses. As for Lee, she felt that the greater the distance she put between herself and Price the better it would be for all concerned. She couldn't rid herself of the shaking feeling she felt inside. Somehow, she was sure that if she had to face Price now, she would fly apart like a broken watch.

Stone Manor looked the same to Lee. The sun touched

the weathered gray stone and gave it a velvet look. The grounds were as green as she remembered them, and she had to smile when Gladdy gasped at the size of the rhododendron bushes along the curving drive leading to the house.

Before the car had fully stopped the front door was flung open and Scylla literally leaped down the steps, flinging herself at Lee. "I have been waiting hours," she squeaked, hugging Lee tightly and laughing. "You look beautiful, not a day older . . . well, not as babyish as you did. Oh, Lee, I have missed you." Scylla sobbed a breath, putting one hand up to her eyes.

"And I've missed you. I haven't been on a decent shopping spree since we parted," Lee teased, blinking against the sudden wetness in her own eyes.

When Scylla discovered Rica, it was love at first sight.

"Do you know where the horses are?" Rica whispered hopefully.

"I certainly do . . . and I know a horse that is just waiting for a big girl like you to ride him." Laughing, Scylla looked up at Lee from her crouched position next to the child. "Thank God she isn't like you, Lee. She likes horses."

Lee grimaced, nodding. All at once everyone was talking at once. Even the staff were grinning from ear to ear as Lee greeted each one personally.

Lee frowned at Frederick when she saw the room that was prepared for Rica. He gave her a sheepish shrug and turned away. It was all flounces in pale yellow and white, the dotted swiss canopy over the bed echoed in the curtains and chair cover. There were stuffed toys on the bed, and as Rica went to sit down on the chair, a yawning puppy crawled out from underneath the bed.

Lee reached for her father-in-law's arm. "You're going to spoil her, you know." She tried to make her voice severe but the happy glint in his eyes as he watched the child and puppy frolic overcame her. She put her arm around Frederick and leaned her head on his shoulder. "It's good to be back, Frederick. I had forgotten how beautiful it is here."

"It's good to have you back, my dear. It was a lonely place without you. Both my son and I found little happiness here when you were gone from us, Lee."

Lee smiled, not wanting him to see her pain at the mention of Price.

CHAPTER EIGHT

Scylla was having a party. She had just jackknifed up on her lounger next to the pool and announced this fact to a sleepy Lee, who was dozing on the brightly colored chaise beside her. The voices of Rica and her grandfather were exuberant as they splashed in the pool.

"Scylla, do be still. There's a good girl. I want to have a nap." Lee yawned behind one hand, her eyelids fluttering as she tried to focus on her vibrant brunette friend in her white Lycra bikini. "If you insist on dragging me on this hunt tomorrow, I want to get some rest."

Actually, Lee had done nothing but rest in the week they'd been at Stone Manor. After spending the first couple of days worrying that Price might arrive at any time, she had succumbed to the peaceful English countryside and allowed her body and mind to relax. She was feeling better every day. The longer Price stayed away the better she would feel, she was sure of that.

Rica was growing browner. These past few days, her happy laughter seemed to echo through the manor's halls. The gardener's granddaughter had become a constant visitor, and her grandfather was never too busy to join in all her schemes. Even Gladdy was finding the stay a happy one, anticipating her nightly chess games with Frederick with glinting relish.

"Oh, Lee, don't be such a fuddy-duddy," Scylla was saying. "It's a perfect idea. You have to go into town to discuss your book with that . . . whatever it is . . ."

"Publishers. That's who it is. They want me to have an autograph party at a book store . . ." Lee smiled wryly at her friend's frowning indifference.

Scylla waved an indolent hand. "Well, whatever it is, you still have to go to town. If Price didn't mind, you could stay with me at Daddy's flat. Then we could have the party that night and drive back here the next day. What do you think?"

Lee's thoughts raced as she slowly nodded. "Yes, that is a good idea. I could stay with you."

Scylla shrugged. "Of course. Price shouldn't mind. After all, he doesn't even bother to come down here and visit. He certainly wouldn't have time for you if you went to town." Scylla pursed her lips in irritation. "You would think he would want to be down here with Rica."

"He calls her every evening," Lee said in fading accents.

"Balderdash," Scylla said flatly. "Why isn't he down here? After the way he raved about her, and you, for that matter, you would think he would have to be with you both every second. I think nothing comes before a man's work," she pronounced in sepulchral tones.

Lee tried to laugh, but it came out sounding like a croak.

"Oh, I'm sorry, Lee." Scylla was contrite. "You no doubt miss the bastard."

"Scylla! If your father heard you using such unladylike language what would he say?"

"Probably he would blame the terrible American influence I've fallen under since you've arrived," she said, mocking amusement lighting her almond-shaped eyes.

"Monster!" Lee laughed, stretching. "Oh, this is nice. Why don't you cancel that fiasco tomorrow. You know I don't ride well and I don't believe in hounding anything, human or animal," Lee said, her lips tightening as she thought of the hapless fox who would be running for his life.

"Now, don't look like that, Lee. I've already told Brad and he'll see to it that you aren't anywhere near the kill."

Lee shuddered, wishing she had never agreed to accompany Scylla and her fiancé on such an outing.

"Besides," Scylla continued, her tones soothing, "you'll be with Sir Oliver Torrance. He'll see to it that you aren't upset. Wait until you see him, Lee. He's a real hunk, as you Americans say."

"This American doesn't say it." Lee laughed at the irrepressible Scylla, but inside she still shivered about going on the hunt. She knew it was an integral part of many an Englishman's life, just as it was for many people in Virginia and Maryland. Still, she couldn't think of it as anything but senseless killing.

The next day dawned bright and sunny and Lee cursed it. "Whatever happened to those foggy, rainy English days," Lee muttered at the blue sky as she stood at her bedroom window. Defeated, she hurried through her shower and donned the riding togs that had been laid out for her. Perhaps it was her imagination, but the hacking jacket felt like armor and the jockey bonnet felt like lead on her head. She affixed the strap under her chin and grasped the riding gloves. She took one more fast look in the mirror, noting her pallor and the tight look around her mouth. She frowned at the gleaming boots and turned to the door, her left hand slapping the crop against her leg.

The orange juice she'd had for breakfast turned to pure acid in her throat as she watched Jackie Pruett, Frederick's trainer, lead the delicately prancing mare toward the mounting block. Lee knew that Lady Fair was considered small amongst her counterparts and almost too docile even though she jumped with eagerness and grace, but Lee felt she was climbing aboard an elephant as she eased into the saddle. She gave Jackie a weak smile and took the reins from his hand.

Scylla trotted up to her, serene and able on a larger, more fiery hunter, introducing the man at her side. "This is Oliver, darling. I told him of your aversion to the kill and he promised me that he would see to it that you were not involved." Scylla smiled, then indicated the other man sidling up on his horse. "And here's Brad. These others aren't important," she stated airily. "You'll meet them all at the breakfast later." With a flip of her hand Scylla turned away to speak to someone else.

"Ah . . . really, you don't have to stay with me, Sir Oliver," Lee began, getting a fresh impression of his chestnut coloring when he smiled. Though his eyes were a pale blue, his skin was deeply tanned, and his brown hair had reddish highlights. She felt her eyes widen as she looked at the glint of amusement in his eyes. Unlike Price's, there was no mockery in them.

"I know that, Mrs. Chatham, but I'd like to." He leaned over his horse's neck, patting it. "Do you think you might call me Oliver?"

Lee nodded, smiling, urging him to call her by her first name.

It took more confusing moments to get the hounds in order and Lee found herself laughing and smiling in a more relaxed way as Oliver exerted himself to entertain her. She almost forgot she was on a horse until the horn sounded and her stomach knotted again. Oliver nodded at her encouragingly and they set off behind the others.

Lee's early fears began to subside as Lady Fair took her easily over the ground, her smooth gait cushioning the ride. She lifted her head to say something to Oliver and glimpsed the fence that the forward group was now taking with incredible ease. Pulling back on the reins she felt the bit sawing the mare's soft mouth and regretted her action. Off to her left she saw Oliver following the pack, taking the fence with room to spare. She knew he hadn't seen her turn away.

Taking a deep breath, she guided the biddable mare down a path, feeling sure she would come up on the pasture at the end of it. To her irritation the path led down to what Lee would have called, at home, a gully. The going was slower here because there were brambles and Lee didn't want any scratches on Lady Fair's glossy coat. She patted the mare's neck and urged her onward slowly. "There's a good girl. Now don't you worry. You won't miss out on the chase. I can hear the hounds. I'm sure they will be coming this way again soon." Lee smiled as the animal whinnied in answer. Looking around at the tangle of growth, she was struck by the rich greenery and the bright colors of the wild flowers. "England is beautiful, isn't it?" she whispered to the horse, not wanting to disturb the sweet serenity of the scene.

A sudden scratching, whimpering sound startled Lady as well as Lee. The horse whinnied in nervous expectancy as she sidled away from the underbrush at the side of the path. Gripping the reins in one hand, Lee leaned over the animal's neck, trying to peer into the thicket, but she couldn't see a thing.

Dismounting slowly, she eased the reins over Lady's head and, step by cautious step, approached the thickly growing scrub. She allowed her hand to slide down the length of the rein as she stretched to see, parting the nettles with a gloved hand. There, almost at her feet, lay a good size fox . . . or maybe it was a vixen, Lee thought wonderingly, as the growling, panting creature stared up at her. Lee was sure it was as panicky as she was. She could tell even by her first cursory glance that the animal had either been mauled by another or had been in a trap and injured itself in its struggle for freedom.

She gasped with fright as the animal moved, her hand jerking on the reins. The already trembling Lady, unnerved by the alien scent of the fox, reared, neighing in fright. Before Lee could turn and take a stronger hold of the horse, Lady bolted, putting her head down and galloping for home.

"Oh, damn, damn, damn," Lee howled, shaking her fist at the departing horse. Then she looked down at the shaking creature at her feet. "Now look what you've done. I shall have to walk." Arms akimbo, Lee shook her head, rocking the jockey bonnet. "And tell me, what am I to do with you. With my luck, you'll probably bite me and you'll have rabies and I'll have to have all those painful abdominal shots." Lee jammed the bonnet down tighter on her head and started to crouch toward the animal. The creature was so exhausted by its ordeal—Lee was sure now that it had been trying to escape the hounds—that it didn't try to lash out at her. Still, it took a great deal of cautious effort before she could finally coax the little beast to remain still while she eased it into the hacking jacket she had removed. The sun was climbing higher as she soothed and cajoled the wild fox, all the time praying that the hounds would not suddenly find the scent again.

Perspiring, struggling up the path that led out of the gully, she kept a firm but not tight hold on the surprisingly heavy animal in her arms. Onward she plodded, in the direction of Stone Manor, she hoped, but she had lost all sense of direction and wasn't sure if she was going the right way. Hunger pangs began as she thought of the hunt breakfast, which would probably be over by now.

She stumbled through a copse of trees onto a road and heard the sounds of horse's hooves galloping toward her. She waited warily, ready to head back to the forest if there were hounds. Up the road Oliver came into view, alone, looking worried as he scanned the forest. The palpable relief on his face when he spied her almost made Lee laugh. "Oliver, I'm so glad to see you. I was getting tired." She tried to grin at him. "Don't rush over to me with that horse. You'll startle my passenger."

Open-mouthed, Sir Oliver listened to Lee's tale, then insisted on dismounting and letting her ride, carefully relieving her of her burden and assuring her that he would be very careful of the injured fox.

It was slow going. The fox was not any more comfortable with Oliver than he was with it. Several times Lee dismounted from Torrance's rangy hunter to soothe the agitated creature. Oliver even made the tentative suggestion that they release it, but Lee was adamant that she would get the animal to a veterinarian. Finally, tired of dismounting from the horse, Lee decided she would walk and carry the fractious animal again and let Oliver lead the horse. Dismounted, she leaned toward him to take the fox and settle it in her arms.

"You cradle it like a baby, Lee." Oliver laughed down at her, giving her shoulder a friendly squeeze.

"Well, it is a baby, in a way. Poor thing. Imagine what it feels like to be a victim of man's amusement." Lee crooned at the staring fox, keeping her face well back in case the creature lashed out. She looked up again at Oliver gratefully. "Thank you for not treating me like a fool."

"Touching." The scathing voice tore between them, making them turn guiltily to face Price.

"I never even heard you coming," Lee blurted, surprised at her husband's appearance.

"No doubt. What are you doing out here?" he barked, not even looking at Torrance. "I raced out here looking for you after I arrived in time for the breakfast and found everyone in a tizzy because you had disappeared and your horse had returned without you. How stupid of me not to have figured that you decided to take the long way home . . ."

"Now, listen here, old man. Your wife has . . ." Oliver began.

"Never mind my wife. I'll take care of her," Price snarled.

"Price Chatham, stop it. You're upsetting the fox," Lee railed, trying to soothe the animal as it pushed against her. "I won't say one more word until I get this creature to the vet's."

"What the devil have you done now?" Price growled in hard amusement as he dismounted from his coal-black stallion and approached her. Lee saw his reluctant smile widen as he looked down at the now-growling fox wrapped in her hacking jacket. "Only you would abscond with the fox. All right, all right, don't rip up at me." He took a deep breath and looked around him, then back at Torrance. "Lead my horse in with yours, will you, Torrance? Tell my father I'm taking Lee to Duncan's place, then we'll take his truck into the vet's. Tell him we'll be back as soon as possible."

Hardly giving Lee time to thank Oliver, Price took her arm and led her up a small knoll. They were at the farm after a short walk. Price seemed to have no difficulty explaining the situation to Duncan. The taciturn farmer even gave Lee a nod of approval as he helped her into the passenger seat of the truck.

They drove the first few miles in silence. Lee leaned over the seat to watch the animal, who reclined in the small space behind the driver's seat. Satisfied that he would ride without too much difficulty, Lee turned around and subsided into her seat with a sigh of relief, beginning to feel the deep tiredness from her long walk.

"I'm sure Duncan will be your friend for life," Price said abruptly. "He has always hated the fox hunts and belongs to an organization that is trying to have them outlawed. I'm afraid they won't have much success in most quarters, but I'm sure Frederick won't have another."

"What do you mean?" Lee questioned him cautiously, not sure of his mood but fully aware that when he had come upon her and Oliver he was in the grip of a terrible rage. *If I didn't know better I would almost think he was jealous,* Lee thought. *What a joke!*

"It seems one of the farm children was describing to Rica how the hounds savage the fox, and when Frederick returned from the hunt she was crying. When I arrived he was white-faced and grim. He promised her there would be no more hunts at Stone. That was when he told me that you hadn't returned yet." He gave a bark of mirthless laughter. "What a fool you must think me! Rushing out there to the rescue when you didn't need me at all."

"I don't think any such thing. It just happened that Oliver came first . . . but . . . but I was still glad when you came. It was much quicker to go to Duncan's than it would have been to walk the horse all that distance to Stone carrying the fox," Lee said weakly, knowing she had said it badly.

"Thank you," Price said bitingly, his hands tensely gripping the wheel.

The rest of the trip was silent. Lee was glad when they arrived at the vet's. He didn't seem in the least disturbed that she had removed the fox from the hunt. In fact Lee could see his lips twitching as he looked at her while Price made the explanations.

Lee caught sight of herself in the mirror on the back of the vet's door. Appalled, she took in the dented jockey bonnet askew on her head, the dirt smudges and scratches on her cheeks. There were dried blood marks on her shirt and long black smears on her fawn-colored jodhpurs. Her boots were mud-spattered and gouged at intervals from toe to top.

I look like I've been through a war, she thought miserably. *No doubt Price wishes he were back in London with all the lovely, gracious creatures he sees night and day,* she thought, grinding in her teeth in jealousy.

"Lee? Lee, listen, will you." Price's voice was curt.

"Yes? Oh, sorry, Doctor Pitt, I didn't mean . . ." Lee shrugged, her face staining red as she looked at the vet's indulgent smile.

"The fox will be fine, Mrs. Chatham. I'll keep it with me for a few days until I'm sure it's stable, then I'll arrange to have it released in a safe area." He paused, clearing his throat, then looked over his half-glasses at Lee. "Ah, you realize, Mrs. Chatham that this creature could be . . . well."

Lee nodded, not looking at Price. "Rabid. Yes I know

that, but it didn't bite me . . . or . . ." Lee felt Price fidget at her side and stiffened.

"Nevertheless," Dr. Pitt continued, glancing nervously at Price, who was clenching and unclenching his fists, a harsh glitter in his eyes, "you must stay in the vicinity until we make sure the animal is healthy. If it is not . . ." He coughed.

Price thrust forward, his hands splaying in front of him. "Yes, dammit, what are you saying? Is my wife in danger?"

"No, I don't think so, Mr. Chatham, but if we find that the animal is rabid, I would recommend the series of shots even though your wife says the animal did not bite her."

"I don't think I need the series, doctor . . ." Lee began.

"My wife will have the shots if there is any question of contagion. You will kindly keep Stone Manor informed of the animal's progress . . ."

"Price, for heaven's sake . . ." Lee sputtered.

". . . and I will see to it that my father is apprised of the situation. Under no circumstances are any chances to be taken. Do I make myself clear?" Price rasped, totally ignoring her.

Before she could say more than a quick good-bye, Price had taken her arm and almost dragged her from the office. He shoved her into the front seat of the truck, his face grim, then went around to the driver's side and slid behind the wheel.

"Do you mind telling me what that little piece of macho action was all about?" Lee hissed, her temper boiling just below the surface.

"Damn you to hell," Price roared, causing Lee to round on him, her mouth agape. "Where do you get off risking your life like that? Why didn't it occur to you that the animal could be rabid?"

"I don't know," Lee yelled back. "Probably the same reason it didn't occur to you."

Price turned toward her in a violent motion, his eyes

murderous. "Do you know the pain you will have to endure if that animal is rabid?"

"Yes. Well, I did think of that . . . its being rabid I mean, but I just couldn't leave it to die. Could I?" Lee asked, her tones placating as she looked at Price's white face.

"No, of course not. It's far preferable that you die yourself, isn't it?" Price laughed mirthlessly.

CHAPTER NINE

Price remained at Stone Manor until the vet assured him that the fox was quite free of disease. It seemed to Lee that he was anxious to return to London, as he left the day after the veterinarian submitted his report.

What did it matter if he left or stayed? she argued with herself, walking through Stone Manor's formal gardens. *Even when he's here, he ignores me,* she mused, leaning over to smell a fully opened blossom that shed its blooms even as she sniffed. *He makes me feel invisible,* she railed in her mind, hurt and anger battling for first place in her thoughts. *The only time he smiles at me is when I'm holding Rica. It will be pretty awkward lifting Rica into my arms when she's a teen-ager just so I can get a smile from my husband. Why do I let him get to me?* She rubbed her fist against her cheek. *Oh, God, why do I have to love this man?*

"What are you doing, Mommy? Are you mad at something?" Rica caroled, skipping down the path toward her, Frederick and Gladdy strolling behind. "Grandpa says I'm to have a pony."

Lee looked back at her sheepish father-in-law and tried to frown at him, but she was so pleased with the glow of health he seemed to have acquired in the short time they'd all been at Stone that she found it hard to be irritated with him. Love can never really spoil anything, she reasoned to herself.

"Scylla says that you're traveling to town with her and

staying at their flat," Frederick said, a quizzical look on his face.

Lee knelt down in front of Rica, rubbing her hand over her daughter's satiny black curls, not wanting to be evasive with Frederick but knowing that she couldn't discuss Price with him. "Uh, yes, I thought I would. I have that meeting with a person called Aranstein . . ."

"Yes, Claude Aranstein." Frederick nodded. "I know him. He's a very clever man. He'll tout your book to its best advantage, Lee. We've used him for years."

"Yes, Price said that he was good." Lee rose to her feet as Rica and the puppy raced down the path. She kept her eyes on the child as she continued. "Uh, Price plans to be very busy this week . . . in and out of the flat constantly. I just thought it would be much simpler if I stayed with Scylla. I can handle my business, then be right on hand to help her with the party that she's planning," Lee explained.

If Frederick's nod seemed doubtful, Gladdy's look was downright disbelieving.

Lee let her eyes slide away from her friend's fixed stare. "Will you and Gladdy be coming into town for Scylla's soiree?" she quizzed lightly, wanting to keep the conversation on keel.

"No, I don't think so," Frederick replied before Gladdy could answer. "Gladdy needs a few more lessons in chess, poor dear."

"Me!" the older woman said scathingly. "I'm not the one who's been in check for two nights running."

"Deep strategy, my dear. I'm lulling you into a false sense of security," Frederick pronounced, his eyes twinkling.

"Twaddle," Gladdy shot back, her lips fighting a smile, and Lee took a deep breath, relieved that no more explanations would be required.

That evening after she had settled Rica in bed and

returned to her own room to shower and dress, there was a soft tap at her door.

"Yes? Come in," Lee called. She had dressed for dinner in a pale blue shirtwaist, a deceptively simple dress that looked severely tailored until one noticed that it was made of multiple layers of gossamer silk that flared with the tiniest movement Lee made.

"You look lovely, child," Frederick said from the doorway as he entered and closed the door behind him, a jeweler's box tucked in one fist.

Lee looked from his hand to his smiling eyes, then shook her head in slow comprehension. "You're spoiling both of us, Frederick."

"No, I'm not." He grinned at her and opened the velvet box. "This belongs to you. It was Price's grandmother's and both my wife and I decided that it should go to Price's wife. Besides, they match your eyes." He lifted a circle of sapphires from a bed of white velvet, the lovely stones flashing in the light of a nearby lamp.

"Oh, Frederick, they're gorgeous. I don't know what to say," Lee gasped, turning to look at the necklace in the mirror as Frederick clasped it around her throat. He handed her the matching drop earrings, and even though they were a bit formal for her dress she quickly put them on. She stood for a moment, smiling into the mirror image of Frederick behind her. "Thank you, I'll treasure them . . . but . . ." she began, swallowing with difficulty.

"No, don't say anything else." Frederick clasped her shoulders, his eyes intently serious as he watched her in the mirror. "I know that you and Price are having problems. Oh, don't look so surprised. It's there for anyone to see, especially someone who loves you both. I'm sure Gladdy has noticed something, but, to her credit, she has said nothing." His hands squeezed her shoulders lightly. "Is there anything you would like to talk about?"

Lee pressed her lips tight to still their trembling and shook her head, her hand coming up to clasp his. "I'm afraid that Price and I are just incompatible." Lee's voice wobbled. Not even to Frederick could she confide that she was sure that Price didn't love her. It was too painful to speak aloud.

"All right, child, just remember that I am here and that I do care about you." Frederick patted her once more, then turned and left the room.

Lee was glad of Scylla's incessant chatter on their trip to the city a few days later.

"Lee, darling, I'm so glad you're going to be staying with me. Our flat is closer to your destination, too. Daddy says the car is at your disposal, but quite frankly I think you'd be better with a cab." Scylla leaned forward to switch down the music, giving Lee a quick glance as she did so. "Lee, you know I would never interfere but it doesn't take a marriage counselor to see that you're quite unhappy. Is it Price? Would you like to talk about it?"

Lee gave the other woman a wan smile. "Yes, it's Price. No, I don't want to talk about it." She put a hand on Scylla's sleeve. "It isn't that I don't want to confide in you, Scylla. It's just that I find it almost impossible to discuss Price with anyone. It's just too difficult."

"I understand. Well, what I mean is, I think I understand. Lee, I have to tell you that in all my life, I have never seen another couple more in love than you and Price were. I don't know what happened to all that beautiful feeling, but I do know that such a oneness is perhaps one of the world's great rarities. I should think it would be worth preserving."

Lee swallowed around the ache in her throat. "Everything changes. People change." She knew she sounded cryptic and uncommunicative but she felt helpless to explain the sense of loss she was already experiencing when she pictured her life without Price.

Scylla reached over and patted her leg. "You're going to have a few hectic days with me. It will be just the medicine you need to perk up your spirits. We shall buy out the stores and give a very lavish party. My father and Price will have to go on the dole when we finish."

Lee laughed at the puckish look on Scylla's face, trying to force Price's image from her mind. She made up her mind she wasn't going to spoil Scylla's fun. She would join in her plans if it killed her.

Scylla's flat was almost as luxurious as the Chathams' and Lee allowed herself to be led from room to room to see it all.

"I think we'll have to throw open Daddy's study the evening of the party. Otherwise it will be a crush, don't you think?" Scylla mused, gazing around the large rectangular room done in Wedgwood green and white with a green, pink, and cream Persian carpet on the floor. The effect was warm and inviting. Lee knew that the Louis Quinze furniture was genuine.

Lee shook her head at Scylla. "How many people do you intend inviting? Fifty people would be more than comfortable in here."

"Oh, I should think there will be twice that number," Scylla said airily, her arm lifting in a sweeping gesture. "Yes, I think I'll have Dodson open up the wall to Daddy's studio and the dining room as well. We'll need the room. Don't laugh, Lee, we'll need the room. Just wait, and stop laughing at me."

The next day was a busy one for Lee. She was late for her appointment with Claude Aranstein because Scylla had so many things to tell her at breakfast.

She practically skidded into the room past the announcing secretary, breathless and flushed. "I'm sorry, I'm late, Mr. . . ." She paused, her mouth wide open as she saw Price sprawled on a couch in front of an electric fireplace, setting down his cup on the coffee table in front of him. He rose to his feet in an easy motion, cocking his head at her.

"Good morning, darling. You've just made a liar out of me. I told Claude you're always on time." As he strolled toward her, she tried not to stiffen, not really thinking he would kiss her in front of this stranger. When he took hold of her upper arms she decided he was going to give her a peck on the cheek.

She gasped with shock as his mouth closed over hers in an open, intimate kiss that shook her to her ankles. When he released her she tried to catch her breath and glare at him at the same time. The glint of amusement in his eyes added to her anger.

"Lee, this is Claude Aranstein. Claude, this is my wife." Price had his arm tight around her waist as he performed the introductions. When Lee tried to wriggle free, the arm tightened even more.

"Mrs. Chatham, this is a real pleasure. I've read your works and found them quite poignant. You have talent."

"Thank you." Lee took the proffered hand, studying the man in front of her, wondering how the dynamo that Frederick had described could be couched in such a short, corpulent body, his tonsured head gleaming as he stood near the desk lamp. His hands were square and somewhat pudgy, his suit a blue and pink Glen plaid that emphasized his roundness.

"Mrs. Chatham, I can't wait to start promoting your book. And, if I do say so myself, I'm the one for the job."

Lee settled herself on the couch and accepted a cup of coffee from Mr. Aranstein's secretary. "I'm sure you are, Mr. Aranstein, but I wish you would call me Lee. I would prefer it." Lee saw the startled look that Aranstein gave Price but pretended not to notice.

"Ah, well, thank you, Mrs. . . . Lee. I hope you'll call me . . . uh . . . Claude. Now, your husband tells me . . ."

Halfway through the conversation, Lee had the feeling that the two men were only including her out of courtesy. Her suspicion grew that the conversation was just a glossed-over repeat of one that Aranstein and Price had had before. She could feel heat rise in her as she realized that Price was manipulating her again, handling all of her business and only pretending that her presence was necessary at these meetings. The heat grew to a slow burn until she hardly heard the words the men were speaking. Neither man seemed to notice when Lee's responses became only monosyllables, then curt nods, then dwindled to nothing.

She rose when Price rose and even allowed him to take her arm as they strolled to the outer office with Aranstein.

"It's been a pleasure meeting you and talking about your work, Lee," Aranstein stated, his voice suave and assured as he took her hand.

"Really? Is that what we did?" Lee smiled widely, noting his puzzled look as she turned to the door. She could hear Price murmuring something but she headed straight for the elevator. If she hurried perhaps she could lose him. "Going down," Lee called just as the elevator doors began to close. She stepped inside and exhaled a deep breath. As she turned, Price was beside her, his mocking eyes looking down into hers. Lee felt smothered. It was all she could do not to lift her fists and pummel him.

When they stepped into the lobby, Price turned to her, his arm sliding around her waist.

Lee pulled herself free, glowering at him. "Don't you *ever* try to sit in on one of my meetings again. I mean that. Who gave you the right to decide what I should do with my work, any phase of it?"

"So that's it," Price drawled, leading her toward his car. "I knew you were boiling about something."

She slammed into Price's Ferrari and they pulled away with a muted roar. Price passed the speed limit in seconds. "All right now, get rid of it. Say what's on your mind."

"I damn well won't have you managing my business as though I was some dumb stuffed animal. I have been handling my work for years without you and I won't tolerate being treated like a fool," she grated, hitting her open palm on her purse. "And take the turn up ahead. I'm staying with Scylla."

"Like hell you are! You're staying at our place."

"No, I'm not. I told Scylla I would stay with her and help her with her party tonight and I'm going to do it."

"You bitch!" Price ninety-degreed his left turn, the tires screeching. "I told you before that I'm not taking this kind of treatment from you, Lee."

She winced at the raw fury in his voice but went back at him just the same. "And I told you that we are divorcing and that I am in charge of my own life. I'm not the zero you seem to think I am and I will not allow you to push me back into the last century just because you think that's where women belong."

"I'm not like that," Price responded, stung by her tone. She knew he was angry, but it puzzled her to think he might be hurt by what she said.

They screeched to a stop in front of Scylla's flat. Lee hurtled forward against her seat belt. She glared at him but he didn't turn his head to look at her. As soon as she had alighted from the car and closed the door, the vehicle shot forward as though it had been fired from a cannon.

Lee closed the door of the flat behind her and headed straight for her room and a bath. She felt her nerves coming right through her skin. God, how awful it was to love someone who didn't love you back! The years stretched ahead like a painful maze. She would be seeing him again and again, she was sure. There would be no way he would be separated from Rica now.

She sighed as she lowered herself into the steaming water and let her body roll to the soothing rhythm of the Jacuzzi. She had no conception of time as she dozed there, letting her body be massaged gently by the moving water.

"Lee? Lee, are you in there?" Scylla's voice penetrated her heat-induced lassitude.

"Yes, I'm here, Scylla. What is it?"

"Darling, did you forget that we had invited a few people to dinner before the others arrived? Our dinner guests will be arriving in less than an hour."

"Oh, Lord," Lee groaned, standing and swishing the water over the edge onto the carpeting surround. "I did forget. I'll hurry."

The dress she chose to wear was not a new one but it was one of her favorites. It was a deep wine silk that swathed her body like a sari, but the hem just touched the knee. Lee coiled her hair low on her neck, the severe style delineating the fine bones of her face. She wore filigreed gold drop earrings interspersed with garnets that were the same deep color as the dress. Her only other jewelry was a high-pronged garnet ring that had belonged to Price's grandmother. Her shoes were strappy sandals in supple wine-colored leather.

Dinner was a hilarious affair. Lee felt confidence flow through her as she reacted to the light-hearted banter of Brad, Oliver, and Scylla. The other couple, Lissa and Eliot Friedman, were long-time friends of Scylla's and Brad's. Lee felt at home with them almost at once.

She felt a twinge of regret when she heard the door chime, announcing the first guests. From that moment it was an unending round of introductions and laughing repartee. Lee could sense her body uncoiling from its tension as Oliver led her to dance.

"Lee, darling, you look beautiful," Oliver whispered into her ear as he pulled her closer to avoid colliding with another couple dancing nearby. "I think I'm in love with you."

Lee looked up at him, blinking her eyes in vaudevillian flirtation. "Oh, Sir Oliver, you'll turn this Yankee's head sure enough." She laughed as he grimaced at her mockery.

"I'm serious, darling. I've been thinking about you all week."

Lee laughed again and rested her cheek against his lowered one.

"Do you mind if I dance with my wife?" Price's cold voice cut between them like a knife, making Lee jump back in Oliver's arms.

CHAPTER TEN

"I say, old man, you startled us," Oliver said, his voice low but no less cold than Price's.

"Did I, old man? Let me tell you again to stay away from my wife . . ."

"Price, for heaven's sake . . ." Lee hissed, noticing that others were listening to the exchange.

Without saying more, Price swept her into his arms. "What did I tell you about Torrance, Lee? I won't have you batting your eyes at other men. You're my wife, and I don't want to hear any more bull about a divorce. I won't listen to it. You're mine."

Sputtering with anger, Lee pulled away from him, going at once to the powder room to repair her makeup and let her temper cool. For the rest of the evening she avoided Price but she could feel his eyes on her from time to time, especially when Oliver was speaking to her. She watched a tall, dark-haired beauty coil herself around Price. Her stomach knotted in impotent fury as she watched him bend toward the statuesque woman Oliver said was called Lettie Tynan.

"Your husband's reputation with women is well known, and the lovely Lettie has been chasing him for some time," Oliver told her. "It looks like she is finally succeeding."

"I'd rather not discuss my husband, if you don't mind," Lee responded, her tones frigid.

The rest of the party was a blur of misery for Lee and she was glad to escape to her room when it was over. Price hadn't even said good night to her, she fumed to herself as she pulled the filigreed garnets from her ears. *He's such a big man! Telling me not to flirt while he drapes himself over that tart. And in New York it was the Juno-esque Darvi,* Lee fulminated, looking at her image in the mirror. *But,* said a quiet little voice in her mind, *it's you he married. It's you he searched for, it's you that he claims as his own. What the hell do you want anyway, Lee Chatham?* The quiet voice was louder now, the image frowning back at her. *What do I want?* Lee questioned herself. *What do I want more than anything? More than writing, more than Highland Farms, more than the loneliness I've had without Price, what do I want? I've loved Rica and Gladdy and I've had happiness with them, but what will fill the void in me?* Lee swallowed, watching the sheen of tears build in her eyes. *I want that man. I want Price, but I'm so terrified of losing him that I run from him, I run from the commitment he offers me because I'm afraid when he finds out how much I love him he'll . . . he'll . . . What will he do, Lee? What will he do? I don't know, I don't know. That's why I'm afraid,* she whispered to the mirror. *Well, you have a choice, that's for sure. Drive him away, and stay in limbo, or fight for him and tell him that you love him and want to stay with him. It's not too late,* the mirror image told her.

Heaving a big sigh, Lee ran to the closet, taking out a pair of dress jeans, old but comfortable, and a white full-sleeved silk blouse that cuffed tight at the wrist. "You look like an out-of-work matador," she mumbled to her mirror image, trying to stem the rising tide of hope in her. "Keep a cool head, lady. Maybe he won't want you anymore. You've certainly told him no often enough."

Leaving a note for Scylla on the front hall table, she picked up the phone and called for a taxi. Fighting the idea that Price might not be home, she climbed into the cab and gave his address, letting the turmoil in her mind surface and take shape. She focused on Price. Even at the beginning, when he first arrived at Highland Farms, though he had been angry with her, he had tried to win her back. Not once had he tried to take Rica from her. Oh, he had threatened it, but then almost at once he said that he had wanted them both. It was true that he was often overprotective, but he was quick to tell her that she had clothes sense, that he enjoyed discussing books, politics, theater, with her. They had often disagreed about these things, but Price had always respected her opinion. Of course, he hadn't taken her writing aspirations seriously, she argued with herself, but she had never really discussed the subject with him. Keeping this one area of her life as her own, she had shut him out of it, even when he inquired about it. She had felt inadequate to be his wife, and so she had kept him at a distance, forcing him with her childish ways to play the role of father rather than husband. Finally, she'd had to get away from him to regain her self-respect, to prove her adulthood to herself, and when Price came back into her life, their relationship no longer worked because she had changed. It was up to her now to set it right, to introduce Price to the adult woman she had become and to show him what only an adult woman could show—that she loved him with all her heart.

She thought of the past, when their love was new. She could almost smell the roses at Stone Manor that summer long ago when she felt Price's supporting arms in the pool. She could sense his protectiveness across the stretch of time. She could almost feel the warm sea water on their honeymoon, his smooth muscled arm enclosing her as she rested against him.

She could still see Frederick standing in the library facing Price when they had come home from London after Price had made her his own.

"You can't marry her so quickly, Price."

"I have married her, Frederick. She is my wife now. I'm taking her to Greece, to the Dodecanese, where mother was born. I'll make her happy." He had caught her close to his side, kissing her temple.

Lee remembered she had blushed as she looked at Frederick, wanting him to understand.

Instead Frederick had glared at Price, before his softened gaze fixed on her. "Did he intimidate you, child? I know my son. Did he steam-roller you into this, Lee?"

Her hesitation at his words had made Frederick's lips tighten. Price had squeezed her tighter, his smile lopsided. "Well, love, did I steam-roller you?"

Lee could still see in her mind's eye the twisted smile Price had given her. She realized now how hurt he had been at her slowness to answer.

"I'm happy, Frederick, truly I am. I'm sorry if you're disappointed about our wedding."

She could still hear Price's harsh laugh as he answered instead of his father. "Darling, don't apologize. You'll convince me as well as my father that you didn't want our marriage."

"Oh, I did . . . I did . . . I did . . . I did . . ."

The words seemed to echo in her mind. *I won't lose you, Price. I'll only leave you again if you ask me to leave. Oh, my love, I don't want it to be too late.*

"Wha' ya say, lady? Here we are."

Lee settled with the driver and hurried into the elevator. Twice she turned away from the apartment door, feeling cold perspiration beading her lip. The third time she inserted the key and stepped into the foyer, listening to the quiet.

With a painful twinge of déjà vu she followed the murmur of voices down the hallway. She could see Price with Felice as she saw them then, six years ago.

The murmured words became clear. "Darling, Price, you know you don't mean that."

Lee heard a smothered oath as though Price had hurt himself.

"Darling, do be careful. However did you trip like that? Did you hurt your toe?"

"Of course I hurt my toe, dammit. Maybe I wouldn't have if you'd stop stalking me around this room. I mean it, Lettie, go home. You had your drink. Now go home. I'm picking my wife up early in the morning and we're going home to see our child. Now, leave."

"That haughty blonde that glared at us all evening? I doubt she'd let you take her anywhere. She doesn't seem to care for you very much, does she?" Lettie's silky tones were malevolent.

"Get out, Lettie." Price's voice was harsh.

Lee took a deep breath and pushed the door wide, seeing the other two turn toward her as though in slow motion. "Yes, Lettie, get out of here."

A mottled red stained through the woman's makeup. "I don't think I'm the one who should leave . . . ah, Lee, isn't it? After all, I was one of the persons who watched your performance tonight with Oliver Torrance . . ."

"How dare you speak to me . . ." Lee began, her fingers curling into her palms.

"Don't take that lady-be-good tone with me," Lettie lashed back.

"I'll do more than talk if you don't leave this apartment in thirty seconds," Lee purred. She watched her husband rather than the incensed Lettie. She watched the emerald eyes open wide, the black eyebrows arching upward. She saw him remove the unlit cheroot from his mouth, the hard glint in his eye becoming amused.

Price lifted the cheroot again to his mouth, the gold lighter flashing at the tip. "Leave, Lettie, my wife seems to be serious." He looked once at the irate woman then back to Lee, smoke curling up his face like a satanic camouflage.

Neither of them noticed Lettie's flouncing exit.

Lee cleared her throat, almost faltering under Price's unflinching stare. "I have something that . . . I want to say." Lee swallowed, her eye watching the cigar ascend to his mouth and stop abruptly. "Right from the beginning I was afraid of losing you. It never seemed real that you loved me . . . It seemed like a dream to be married to Price Chatham. To love a man like that and have him love me back was a fantasy. When I saw you with Felice Harvey I had to run. I couldn't bear to wait and hear you tell me that you loved another woman. In those years we were apart, I used to have nightmares of you telling me you didn't love me. Common sense would suggest that I talk it out with you, but I had no common sense where you were concerned. I still haven't any . . . but I have to tell you how I feel. Then if you don't want us to be together at least you can tell me face to face. I'm older now and I hope tough enough to take it." She tried to smile but her face was too stiff. "But if you decide we should be together, then I have to tell you that some parts of me will never change. If I see you with another woman, I'll seethe and want to lash out. If I find you with another woman . . ."

"You won't," Price interrupted, his voice terse.

"If I find you with another woman," Lee continued doggedly, "like I did with Felice and Lettie, I'll hate it. I'll never trust a woman around you." She cleared her throat painfully. "I might even hit her with a brick or something . . ."

"A lady like you?" Price quizzed, a threat of laughter in his voice.

"I don't feel like a lady when I see another woman with you. Anyway, I want to tell you that I'll still believe in you. I'll believe what you tell me . . ."

"Even when you see women in my bedroom like this?" he queried, his tones silky.

"Yes. I love you, Price. I know other women chase you but . . ."

"And I damn well tried to chase other women, Lee." He watched her wince. "Oh, I tried very hard to forget you with other women, but nothing helped. You were always there, the little girl who took over my life." He took her hand, bringing her palm to his mouth, feathering the sensitive skin with caresses, never taking his eyes from her. "I love you in those tight pants, love, but wouldn't you be more comfortable with fewer clothes on?"

"Yes, I would." Lee gulped, taking a step backward. "But, first, I want to finish what I came to say."

Price's eyes narrowed as they ran over her, his lower lip taking on a more sensual curve. "Maybe I can be patient."

"Will you forgive me, Price? I've been a fool, but I do love you." Lee tried to smile but her face felt frozen.

"I don't know what you want forgiveness for, but you have it. I can forgive you anything because I love you," he said simply.

Tears welled in her eyes and she swiped at them with a shaking hand. "I have realized more and more since your return to me that I was very stupid to do what I did. I know now what a precious thing we have between us, what a rare delight the feeling is! I'm not making excuses for myself, Price. I was young and I loved you so much it scared me. I was still hurt from my father's death when we married and very unsure of myself. That night I saw you with Felice, I couldn't think straight. I forgot all the beautiful moments we had shared and saw only what to me was obvious, that you preferred another woman to me . . ." She let her fingers rub across his lips as she watched his eyes darken with emotion.

"If you had ever known how innocent my meeting in the flat with Felice was you would have laughed, instead of run. But you didn't give me much of a chance to explain, did you darling?"

"No, I didn't. . . ."

Price caught her close as her words trailed into a sob, his tongue trailing down her cheek.

"Then after I was gone from you, I found out about Rica. I thought you might take her from me. After all, I had deserted you." She shuddered against him, wanting him to continue stroking her.

"Do you think you were the only one who was afraid?" Price whispered, his arms tightening as she tried to pull back and look at him. "Lee, baby, if you only knew what you did to me when you were a mere teen-ager, you'd understand why I treated you as I did. You bowled me over when you were just a child . . . so I avoided you. Then a few times I was alone with you and I could feel myself becoming aroused when you smiled at me. You were an innocent, not yet a woman, but I wanted to make the most passionate love to you. God, I hated myself."

"Is that why you were so cutting and cruel to me?" Lee whispered, letting her fingers twine into the curling hair at his nape, tugging it gently.

"Yes." Price's voice was ragged. "That time when you begged me to take you sailing and you wore that pink bikini, I almost blew my top."

"You kissed me for the first time that day." Lee smiled dreamily. Then she frowned. "But you hated it, you were furious with me."

"Yes, I was furious with you. Don't you remember what you said to me?" Price said through his teeth.

Lee looked at him, her brows arching in wonder as she sensed his rising temper. She shook her head, puzzled, trying to remember. "Let me think. You kissed me once. Then you kissed me again. Oh, I think I know what you mean . . ." Lee looked at him, amusement lighting her face. "That bothered you? I don't believe it."

"Believe it. When I asked you how you liked me kissing you and you said that you liked it, that you always liked kissing, I could have strangled you. It had never occurred to me that others might have kissed you before me." Price smiled ruefully, hot color staining his face. "That really rankled. I wanted to kiss you helpless then."

"Instead, you picked me up and threw me in the sea." Lee bit at his ear.

"You were lucky I didn't drown you. At that moment I could have." Price's voice was husky as he continued to stroke her, not troubling to hide the fierce heat in his eyes. "I hated being the bait in a fifteen-year-old's trap. It made me furious to think of you knowing how I felt about you, then laughing about it, maybe to your friends . . ."

"I wouldn't have done that. I couldn't have been that cruel. You should have known that about me," Lee soothed.

"No, I didn't know that about you. I think that's been the core of the trouble all along. We hide from each other, Lee. Neither of us wanted the other to know how we felt." Price's large hand swept the hair off her forehead. He leaned down to follow his hand with his mouth. "After that vacation in Greece, I went out of my way to avoid you. I congratulated myself that I had handled that foolish infatuation quite well. Then I went down to Stone Manor the summer you were twenty and saw you again. The feeling was stronger than ever. I was happy when you contracted the flu because it kept you in England near me. When your father was killed, I tried to back off, give you time. I admit my motives weren't entirely unselfish. I liked my life. The sophisticated women who moved through it knew the rules of the game."

"I remember the women," Lee said, her voice tart.

He gave her a lopsided smile. "I liked my freedom and I had no intention of marrying for years. It was always in the back of my mind that when I did marry it would be someone with the same worldly leanings that I had. I struggled against involving myself with a dewy-eyed virgin fresh from the schoolroom, especially one who looked like a Dresden doll. Ouch, that hurts!" Price winced, as Lee bit his earlobe.

"I hope it hurts, you nasty macho man," Lee purred, rubbing herself against him.

"God, I'm married to a siren," Price breathed, his voice hoarse. He took a deep breath and put both hands on her shoulders, setting her back from him. "You're going to hear this . . . all of it, because after tonight all that I'm telling you now will be ancient history and not too important to our lives, but you must hear it all. We're clearing the air, once and for all, Lee. There will be nothing between us ever again, I promise you that." He looked down at her, a dark smoldering in his green eyes. "After our talk there will be even less between us. I intend to undress you, my love, and keep you in that bed for a few days."

"Days?" Lee laughed breathlessly, reaching a hand out to him again.

"No, stay where you are, Lee. I'm going to finish telling you about a man who was so crazy about you he couldn't see straight."

"Oh, Price, darling, me too," Lee gulped.

Price's face was somber as he drew his index finger down her cheek. "I never counted on the power you had over me, the pull of that delectable body, the cornflower eyes, the tiny nose sniffing with disdain every time you glanced my way, which wasn't often."

"It was a very good act." Lee grinned. "I adored you but I wanted to prove to you that you meant nothing to me, that I was disgusted with you. You were a horrid womanizer and I wanted that horrid womanizer to look at me, to make love to me."

"Damn you, Lee, don't look at me like that," Price grated, taking a quick turn around the room, then returning to stand spread-legged in front of her, a good arm's length away. "All my instincts told me to run, that I couldn't have those feelings about you, but even then I think I knew it was too late." Price gave a harsh laugh, his index finger reaching out to touch her parted lips.

Lee sensed that it was difficult for him to bare his soul to her in such a fashion.

"I was swept away when you gave me your first real smile. I drowned in those blue eyes. I wanted to hold you, protect you. I hated any man who looked at you. I was jealous when my own father held you and comforted you. Paramount was my fear that you would discover those feelings I had for you and be disgusted, turn away from me. I couldn't handle that, so I played it as light as I could . . ."

"You treated me like a baby, like a cuddly toy," Lee replied, not caring about that now because she was beginning to know the depth of Price's love for her. She felt light and carefree, yet strong and sure of herself.

"I rushed you into marriage because I was afraid of losing you. Then I lost you anyway." Price's voice was raw with remembered pain.

Lee ignored his efforts to keep her at bay and reached her arms around his waist, stroking his back comfortingly.

"Do you remember our wedding night? Our first night together?" he whispered, his arms closing around her as though he had no control over them.

"Yes, of course I do, Price. I relived that night a million times when I was separated from you. I hugged the memory like a blanket."

They clung together, mouths fusing, hands clutching each other.

Price leaned back from her, taking a ragged breath. "I knew that I should have waited, given you time, wooed you, proposed to you at a later time, with candlelight and wine, but I was afraid. I wanted you for all my life. That shook me to my socks. The next morning I badgered Clive Ralston to get a special license, any way he could. When I hung up the phone and went back into the bedroom you were still sleeping. I sat there watching you, manufacturing reasons why we should be married at once and not wait. My God, little love, I wanted to weep like a baby when you acquiesced at once." He smiled down at her, his mouth a rueful twist. "I suppose that was one of the reasons for treating you like a doll. I felt I had to keep it light, not let you know how much I needed you. You might have been repelled. I see now I did it all wrong. I should have talked to you, told you of my feelings."

Lee nuzzled his cheeks with her lips, wanting to comfort him. "And I should have talked to you, told you how I adored you, how in awe of you I was. You were so sophisticated, so debonair, so very intelligent. I felt like the president of your fan club, not your wife."

Price slid his hands up her body, awakening every nerve end, his whispered voice harsh in her ear. "I was even jealous when I found out you had a baby and I wasn't there to watch your body grow and change. I could have torn Lieber apart because he saw you then . . ."

"Perhaps he saw me then, I'm not sure, but Grant never started coming to the house until after Rica was born." Lee tried to placate him, wanting to laugh when his face looked even more thunderous. "Darling, don't be silly. That's all behind us now."

"Is it? I wonder if I'll ever get over not having been with you when Rica was born. How lonely it must have been for you!" Price grated, his fingers digging into her.

"It was hard and lonely, but I grew then, Price, I began to realize how deep my love was for you. I used to play a game with myself, working extra hard to see how long I could keep you from my mind. I always congratulated myself if it was a whole day, but never, ever was I able to keep from thinking of you through the nights. Your face was always in my mind when I went to sleep. I just accepted it as a way of life," Lee croaked.

Price was nodding as though he empathized with all she said. "Yes. The worst was when I would be walking down a busy street in London or New York and I would see a diminutive blonde walking along, sometimes on the other side of the street. The times I've run out into traffic or darted in amongst people trying to get to you, only to find it wasn't you." He feathered her cheeks with soft kisses, his heart thudding against her breasts. "Then I walked into Alma's that night totally unaware! You would think

I would have sensed that something astonishing was going to happen. In fact, I was thinking of Darvi when I spotted you in that mirror across the room."

"Damn the woman and drat you for being with her," Lee said, lightly dragging her nails down his cheek.

"Darling, you can claw me to death. All you'll do is turn me on more than I already am." Price gave a mock growl, pressing his face into her nails. "Anyway, you knocked me off my pins that night. After I found you had left with Blaylock, all I wanted to do was find you, but I was weak as a kitten. I collapsed in the hallway on my way to the elevator. I wanted to kill Darvi and Alma for taking me to the hospital. I was sure I had lost you again."

Lee felt a shudder go through him as he tightened his hold on her. As though the pain he felt was seeping into her, her mind began to focus on the torture they had heaped upon each other.

"I can't believe we've had this talk, Lee. It's been like peeling away all the misunderstandings and misconceptions we've had about one another, layer after layer." He pulled back from her, a dull red patching his cheekbones. "I don't think I've ever had such a deep talk in my life. I feel pounds lighter and inches taller."

"Me too, me too," Lee gulped, in delighted awe at the way their minds were in tune.

Price rained soft kisses down her cheek. "Now, I think we've talked long enough. I have other things I'd rather do."

"What might that be?" Lee quizzed, feeling her body glow under his narrowed stare.

"We're going to get to know each other again. You don't think it's too late for that, do you, wife?" Price murmured, his one hand gently kneading her breast.

"It's not too late for us," Lee answered, correctly interpreting his question. "It could never be."

"We'll bathe each other, cook for each other, love each

other . . . and keep on talking to each other. No one, nothing, will come between us again."

"Now you're talking too much, husband," Lee choked, unbuttoning his shirt.

Price swept her up into his arms, his purposeful strides taking them to the bed.

Lee felt as though she had bird wings beating in her throat. She wanted to tell him that she felt as if it were the first time for them, that her life was starting now.

"Darling Lee." Price's lips probed her throat as he stretched beside her on the bed. His lips probed her throat as he stretched beside her on the bed. His blazing eyes roved over her as he undressed her in slow, deliberate motions. "God, I've wanted you, I've wanted to see you like this, beside me. I'll never have enough of you. For me it will always be the first time."

"Me too, me too." Lee repeated herself.

"I've never known you to be so agreeable." Price smiled down at her, the muscle jerking at the corner of his mouth the only facial clue to his excitement. He smoothed the blouse from her shoulders, then shifted her slightly to lift it from her. "No bra. You came through the city that way?" His mouth touched the rosy peaks of her breasts.

"Lots of women don't wear bras today. I'm sure you know that," Lee gasped as he stroked her. "As for being so agreeable . . . well, if you keep doing what you're doing, I'll be a pussycat." She tried to laugh but it came out a moan. Her last thought before she became mindless under his touch was that life stretched out in front of them like a golden path, with no obstacle insurmountable, no problem unsolvable. She was loved and loved back. Nothing was more important.

LOOK FOR NEXT MONTH'S
CANDLELIGHT ECSTASY ROMANCES™

A Candlelight Ecstasy Romance™

"YOU'RE MY WIFE, LEE. DON'T FORGET THAT. I DON'T."

Before she divined his intention, he had crossed the space between them, grasping her wrist and pulling her off balance into his arms. She was fastened tightly to him before she could do more than gasp. Shivering, she tried to pull away, but Price's arms tightened, holding her close to his length. When she heard him chuckle, she tried to wrench free without success.

"This is where you belong, Lee," he muttered, his hard kiss taking her breath away.